WILDEST DREAMS

A MAGNOLIA ROW NOVEL

ANNA MAY

Rose House, LLC

For Will

KENDALL

"*T*he rumors are true."

I look around the monitor of my computer to see my best-friend-since-high-school/secretary, Patsy, standing in my office door. She's bursting with excitement, bobbing up and down on her toes and making her long bleached-blonde ponytail swing like she's a teenager instead of a thirty-year-old mother of five.

"What rumors?" I ask. "This town is so full of them it's hard to keep up."

"Duh. The rumors about the big movie filming here."

I roll my eyes. "Why would Hollywood come to Magnolia Row?" It seems like a fair question. This town is about as dead as a rose in winter.

Patsy looks at me like I've lost my mind. "Um, because this town is beautiful, Kendall. Go outside. Take a look around every now and then."

She has a point. Growing up here, it's easy to forget the streets lined with magnolia trees, the riverside dotted by oaks draped with Spanish moss, and dozens upon dozens of historic mansions make for a picture-perfect Alabama postcard. To top it off, all that Southern charm is compounded by the fact that the town sits on the picturesque Florablanca River at a point where the water widens into a lake large enough for ski competitions and competitive bass fishing.

Honestly, though, it's hard to see the beauty when I've been a bit of a cynical recluse since my divorce three years ago. I pretty much spend all my days either behind my computer at work, where I serve as one of the town's only accountants, or in the apartment above my office, streaming true crime shows. Most days, it's hard to imagine anything exciting happening here, much less a movie production.

"How do you know for sure?" I ask Patsy, who still has the energy of a kid at Christmas. "Did you see Chris Pine walking down the street or something?"

She rolls her eyes and smiles, showing off the charming little gap between her two front teeth. "No, a girl at my church works at city hall. A major production company came in and got all kinds of permits. They even have permission to shut down Main Street for a whole week."

I raise my eyebrows. "Interesting. I guess I'll be stuck here then."

"That's it? You're not excited? Your office may be in an f-ing movie! We can be extras!" In high school, Patsy had the mouth of a sailor. Since giving birth to her first son ten years ago, she's replaced curse words with their abbreviations.

I shake my head. "You can be an extra. I have work to do."

"It's not even tax season!" She waves her arms with exasperation. She means well, and I know she wants to see me get out more, but I don't have the energy. Besides, this has to be another crazy rumor completely fabricated by a bored housewife with nothing else to talk about on the playground, like the rumor that Chick-Fil-A is opening a restaurant here or that Taylor Swift bought a vacation home on the river. These stories are never true. Nothing exciting happens here. Never has, never will.

"Look, when I walk outside and there's a camera crew, I'll believe it. Until then—"

"Whatever. You don't go outside! You won't even see them! You'll be hiding in your office or upstairs watching serial killer shows."

"That's not true!" I argue. "Sometimes I go to the grocery store."

Patsy shakes her head. "You're impossible, Kendall Abbey."

Two weeks of Patsy's non-stop speculation about the movie go by before I finally believe her.

It's Friday morning, which means Patsy is late. Granted, she's always late, but as the week progresses, she gets later and later. On Fridays, I'm lucky to see her by lunchtime. She gets a pass because she's my best friend and, with five young boys at home, she gets tired. As a childless woman, I can only imagine.

The phone rings and I answer in my perky, not-depressed-and-alone, happy-to-help voice.

"Hi. I'm calling about a rental property in Magnolia Row?"

"Yes! The house on the lake?" This takes me by surprise. I had listed the house for rent online after my divorce, but for three years there's been little to no interest in it. Maybe I set the price too high, but it was my dream house. I can't get rid of it, but I also can't bring myself to walk in the door. My heart would break all over again.

"That's right. Is it still available? I'm with Sister Star Productions. We're shooting a film nearby and would like to rent it for one of our actors. It would only be for a few weeks."

"Oh my God." I drop my professional tone and the words spill out of my mouth before I can regain my composure. "Is this a joke?" Patsy will never let me live it down if this is true.

"Excuse me?" The lady on the end of the line clearly thinks I'm an idiot or, at the very least, extremely rude.

"Yes, sorry." I close my eyes and shake my head. "It is available."

"Great! Send over your prices and contract and we'll have a look at it."

"Of course." I get her email address and phone number. The next thing I know, I have an executed short-term lease and $5,000 transferred into my bank account.

Patsy finally drags in, carrying coffee and two turkey

sandwiches from Bread Crumbs. I stand in the entryway of my office, leaning on the frame with arms crossed and a huge smile as she sets everything down on the front desk.

"That's a happy face!" said Patsy. "Did F-er get hit by a truck or something?" Tucker is my ex, but she refuses to call him by his name. Suffice it to say, she's not a fan.

"No, but you're about to give me the biggest I-told-you-so of your life."

She gives me a curious look and waits for my explanation.

"Not only were you right about the movie," I start as her face lights up, "but the production company is also renting my lake house for one of the actors."

She squeals so loud I think my eardrum may burst. "F me. This is so f-ing exciting! I can't wait to tell Garion!" I know Garion, her husband, couldn't care less about movie stars in Magnolia Row, but I guess she has enough excitement for them both. "Who is it? Is it someone we know?"

I chuckle. "We don't actually *know* any movie stars."

"You know what I mean. Is it someone huge? Is this like a movie-movie or a TV movie? Or a Netflix movie? Maybe HBO? I have so many questions!"

"I have no answers. They didn't say and I didn't ask. All I know is that this mystery person will be here in two weeks and will stay for six to eight weeks after that."

She squeals and claps like a little kid.

I simply shake my head. "Since we're not busy right now, I'll need your help getting the house ready. Can you go dust, vacuum, and make sure the linens are clean?"

"Absolutely. I may install a camera or two while I'm there."

"Patsy!"

She's joking.

I hope.

It's the morning the keys are supposed to be picked up and Patsy is in my apartment before I even go down to the office. My apartment, which had served as a storage room when my dad owned the accounting firm I now run, is about as basic as living spaces come. It's an efficiency loft with a tiny bathroom, kitchenette, high ceilings, and tall, thin windows overlooking Main Street. I've done very little in the way of decorating, so the walls are flat white with only a few random trinkets here and there.

I'm still getting ready when Patsy lets herself in. I'm surprised she's actually wearing make-up and her hair is not in a ponytail.

"My mom is taking the kids to school this morning," she says, watching me brush my teeth. "She's as excited as I am! What if Reese Witherspoon walks in the door today?"

I spit out my toothpaste. "Then we can say we've met Reese Witherspoon. My life will go on the same."

"The suspense is killing me!"

After vetoing five of my "boring" outfits, she makes me wear a sundress I'd forgotten I owned and sandals that blister my feet. It's definitely a change from my normal bland office clothes, but I go with it because I don't have the energy to argue this early in the morning.

We walk down the narrow stairs to the office and wait.

And wait.

Finally, two hours after lunch, a petite blonde with bobbed wavy hair comes in the front door. My workspace is essentially three rooms: the front lobby where Patsy sits, my office behind her, and a bathroom under the stairs leading up to my apartment. Because it's tiny, I can hear everything that happens even if I'm hiding behind my computer, so when she walks in, I get up and meet her in the lobby.

This has to be the person picking up the keys, as she's definitely not from here. For one, I don't recognize her. Second, she's wearing a hoodie with tight jeans and Skechers, which is way too much clothing for such a warm May afternoon in the South. Patsy does a poor job hiding her disappointment. This is not a celebrity.

"May I help you?" I ask.

"My name is Harriett. I'm here to pick up the keys to the rental house," she says.

"Of course." I retrieve the envelope from my desk drawer and Patsy wastes no time quizzing her.

"Are you the one staying in the house?" she asks, her voice a few notches higher than normal as she tries to stay calm.

"No, I'm a personal assistant. My boss asked me to pick up the keys for him."

"Who is your boss?" asks Patsy, completely losing all sense of propriety.

"Patsy!" I say, embarrassed as I emerge from my office with the keys. "I apologize," I say to the stranger in my lobby.

"It's fine," Harriett responded, eyeing Patsy. "He's very private. We would appreciate it if that privacy is respected."

"Absolutely," I respond. Patsy nods her head.

I clear my throat. "The key opens both the front and back door. Be sure to tell your boss the back door locks automatically, so he'll have to have the key to get in from the deck."

"Will do. Anything else?"

"Nope! My business card is in there with the keys in case he needs anything."

"Thank you. I'm sure he'll be fine."

With that, she turns and walks out the door.

Patsy looks at me with raised eyebrows. "She was a b."

"She was doing her job."

"All she told us is that it's a man!"

I roll my eyes and go back to my office, ignoring Patsy's phone calls to everyone she knows, telling them about our brief encounter with the assistant to a mystery celebrity.

PIERRE

*H*arriett meets me at the Atlanta airport early on Saturday morning. She's flying back to Los Angeles as I'm arriving in the South. It's a hot, humid day, especially for May. It's been years since I filmed a movie in this area — I had forgotten how sticky it is.

"You've got to be burning up," I say, noting her hoodie with jeans and giving her a hug.

"I'm alright," she says.

"How is the place?" I ask. She had traveled ahead of me to get everything set up.

"It's, uh…"

"Bad?"

She shakes her head. "The house is very nice. Clean. The back is all windows and it has a great view of the river. It's just in the middle of nowhere."

"Fantastic!" I need a break from LA. I need a break from photographers. I need a break from traffic, from the industry, from constant scrutiny, from…well…everything in my life. One of the reasons I agreed to do this movie is because my agent said it's a rural shoot.

"You think that now. Once you leave Atlanta, there's basically nothing for three and a half hours. Not even cell service. It's mostly back roads and farms."

"As long as the GPS works, I'm golden."

She hands me the car keys and an envelope. "This has the keys to the house and the owner's card. She said the back door locks automatically. That's about it."

I open the envelope and look at the business card: Abbey Accounting with a little abacus on the side. I put the keys and card in my pocket.

"Are you sure you don't need me to stay with you?" Harriett asks. As far as assistants go, she's the absolute best. In fact, she may be the only true friend I have in LA.

"No, go home to your hot girlfriend. I'm actually kind of looking forward to not talking to anyone until filming begins. Do you happen to know where Marina is staying?"

Harriett makes a face. "I'd forgotten about that."

Marina Breton is going to be my co-star. We did another picture together years ago and to say she had a crush on me would be an understatement. She had basically stalked me outside my trailer. I changed my number multiple times after that film wrapped, but she still managed to track down each one and blow up my phone. It took a year for her to lose interest. I'm hoping she's still over it, but that may be blind optimism on my part.

When I'd first signed onto this project, another actress was set to play my love interest, but she backed out two weeks ago and somehow Marina's agent got her in to be the replacement. If I'd known Marina was going to be here earlier in the process, I probably would've tried to get out of it too.

To make things worse, a few days ago the publicist for the movie sent me an email, saying she wants us to have a faux rekindled romance to drum up publicity on social media. It's simply not going to happen.

"I wish I'd forgotten about it," I say.

"I have no idea where she's staying," says Harriett, shaking her head and squinting in the bright Georgia sun. "Sorry."

I give her another hug and we part ways. I load my suitcase into the back of my rental SUV, connect my phone to the car and, for the next three and a half hours between Atlanta and southern Alabama, there is nothing in my life besides a classic rock playlist and the wind in my hair.

*M*agnolia Row is beautiful. It's early afternoon when I drive across a bridge over the Florablanca River and the town immediately transports me back in time. The median of Main Street is a solid line of massive magnolia trees in full bloom. The shops along the street look like a Hollywood set from the 1950s and everything smells like barbeque. My stomach howls.

It's clear why I'm here. This is the perfect place to film a movie.

I turn onto River Avenue and pass about thirty houses built in the late 1800s, all in pristine condition with lawns manicured more perfectly than a lot of golf courses. Azaleas surround almost every one and each porch is outfitted with rocking chairs and ferns. It's so stunning I have a hard time focusing on driving.

I slowly make my way north of town and turn into a neighborhood running alongside a wide inlet branching off the main river. My rental is the house in the cul-de-sac and has a magnificent view of the wide, sparkling lake.

I pull into the drive and get out. The lots on this street are spacious with plenty of pine and oak trees, so even though I'm in a neighborhood, I feel secluded.

The house looks brand new, craftsman-style with a back yard that slopes downhill to the water. It has a huge front porch with rocking chairs, and I can see a second-story deck peeping out from the rear. This is exactly what I'd imagined when the studio assured me I'd have a nice, quiet place to relax while I'm not on set. I feel rejuvenated just thinking about sitting on the back porch with a beer and a good book.

I grab my suitcase and go inside, placing the house keys on the counter. It's an inviting space with an open floor plan, marble countertops, plush leather furniture, and a striking view of the water. I stand for a few minutes and take in the view. Pontoon boats dot the glittery horizon of the river and Spanish moss is dancing in the lazy late spring breeze. It's so quiet, and the sky is as clear as clean water.

This is the opposite of LA.

I love it.

*A*fter unpacking, I fix a glass of ice water and walk out onto the back deck to take in the view. The door shuts behind me and I take a sip of my drink before closing my eyes and lifting my face to the sun, breathing deep.

There's a dock with a bench on the riverbank, so I walk down the deck steps and make my way to the water.

Suddenly, I see movement out of the corner of my eye. I turn, thinking there may be a deer or large dog by the trees at the edge of the property.

But no. It is not a deer. Or a dog. Or anything I want to see.

It's an alligator. And it's massive.

The gator emerges from the tree line with a determined stride, coming straight towards me.

Panicked and clearly out of my element, I turn and run as fast as I can, briefly tripping over a tree root before stumbling up the stairs of the deck. Luckily, there's a gate on the landing so I have something between me and the massive beast slowly closing the gap between us. I run across the deck, my heavy steps beating the wood, and try to turn the knob on the back door. It doesn't budge.

Shit. Shit. Shit.

Harriett said the back door locked automatically. She told me that. And as soon as she said it, I forgot. Now I'm stuck on the deck with an alligator in the yard waiting to eat me. As it turns out, quiet country life may not be for me after all.

I fumble through my pockets and pull out my cell phone, then stare at the blank screen like an idiot.

Who do I call? Do police come for alligator emergencies? Or animal control? Does a town this small even have animal control? What the hell am I supposed to do? Wait for it to go away?

I look over the rail. The alligator is still looking at me from the bottom of the steps. It has no intention of leaving, and its massive teeth give the impression that I'd make a good afternoon snack. Luckily, the deck's gate is a barrier, but that doesn't change the fact that I'm stuck.

A white card on the wooden floor catches my eye and I remember I have the homeowner's number. I pick it up with shaky hands and dial.

"Hello?" The voice on the other end of the phone sounds like a teenager.

"Hi, um, I'm trying to reach Kendall Abbey?" I say, reading the name on the card.

"That's me. Who is this?"

"Um, I'm renting a house from you."

"Oh! Hi." She sounds confused.

"Yeah, um… I have a situation. I'm not sure what to do." I try to steady my voice, but it's no use.

"What's wrong?" she asks.

"There's an alligator in the backyard," I blurt out.

"Oh! That's Bertha."

The alligator has a name. Of course it does. She doesn't even sound surprised or remotely concerned.

"Okay, well, Bertha has trapped me on the back deck, and I don't have the key on me so I can't get back in. Is there an animal control for me to call, or do I—"

"No, no, no," she says. "There's one animal control guy and he's, like, eighty years old. Don't do anything. I'll be right over."

My stomach drops. I don't need a young girl to rescue me. Nor do I want photos of me hiding from an alligator to show up online. For all I know, she could use this to earn a quick buck selling pictures to a tabloid.

I shake my head. This will be on TMZ by tomorrow morning. I just know it.

"You don't have to—"

"No, really. I can handle Bertha. Hold tight. I'm on my way."

"Am I safe? I have the deck gate closed."

"Probably."

Probably is not yes.

I'm going to die.

I'm going to die and photos of an alligator carrying my body to the river will be all over the internet until the end of time.

"I'm leaving now. Don't move."

"Don't worry. I won't." I can't. There's ten-foot-long alligator looking at me like I'd make an excellent dinner.

She hangs up and I watch Bertha stalk back and forth across the yard. The sun is high and I start sweating through my shirt.

So much for country life. I'm a joke. Harriett was right. This is what I get for thinking things would be better outside LA.

After what seems like an hour, but is probably closer to fifteen minutes, a small Audi SUV comes flying down the driveway and stops in the back yard, a cloud of dirt trailing behind. The sunroof opens and out pops a tiny woman with long chestnut hair, holding what looks like a small basketball.

"Bertha!" she yells in a cute, mousey voice. This scene is so absurd that I can't help but laugh to myself.

She unwraps the little package and I realize it's a chicken - a small rotisserie chicken.

Bertha, like a trained dog, makes her way toward the SUV and the girl rears her arm back and hurls the chicken across the yard towards the river. Bertha responds, turning her attention to the meat rolling down the hill and close the water. She takes it in her mouth, swallowing it in one gulp, and walks away.

I breathe a sigh of relief and look back as the woman frantically gets out of her car. She's little, barely clearing five feet tall, and wearing pajama pants, flip-flops, and a t-shirt from Auburn University. I unlatch the deck gate and make my way down the steps as she runs towards me, apologizing profusely. She's older than I thought she was from judging her voice—maybe late twenties? Early thirties? Either way, she's beautiful and I'm humiliated.

"I'm so sorry," she says. "I can't believe she's still here. No one has lived in this house—"

I raise my hands to cut her off. "It's okay. I just wasn't expecting an alligator."

We meet in the middle of the sloping back yard. I run my hands through my hair and realize she's frozen, staring at me.

And here it comes: the first embarrassment of recognition.

"Oh my god," she says, her face blanching. "You're Pierre Chatham."

*P*ierre.

Pierre Chatham.

Pierre Chatham is living in my house. Standing in my yard. It might as well be Brad Pitt. Never in my wildest dreams did I image someone like this would be renting my house.

I'm here, in front of Pierre Chatham, with no makeup, wearing mismatched pajamas and flip-flops. Not to mention that my hands are covered in rotisserie chicken grime.

What. A. Nightmare.

He's...well...he's exactly what you would expect a movie star to look like. Tall, lean, broad shoulders, piercing blue eyes, and messy, dirty blond hair. He's older than me, but not by much. He has fine lines around his eyes and his skin is slightly weathered, but he wears it well. I could go on, but the more I think about how perfect he looks, the more I realize how imperfect I look.

Humiliation? Mortification? No. The English language lacks the word for how completely stupid, surprised, and horrified I feel. I want to crawl into a hole and die.

"I'm so sorry," I say again. This apology is not for Bertha, but for myself. For the stupefied look on my face. For blurting out his name like he's a thing instead of a person. For clearly making him uncomfortable.

He shakes his head. "No, you're fine. I'm just happy the alligator is gone."

We stare at each other for a moment, not saying anything. What do you say to a movie star? I want to act normal, but I'm too awkward and can't think of anything to talk about, so I simply stand with my mouth hanging open and wiping my hands on my pants like a toddler.

"Did you want to come in and wash your hands?"

My stomach drops. I haven't been in the house since the divorce and I have no plans to go back inside anytime soon.

"No," I say, looking down at my feet. My toenails aren't even painted. Ugh. I'm a mess. "I'm good."

"So," he says with a sly grin that cuts the tension, "can I expect Bertha to visit often or…?"

I laugh and he looks down at me with an amused expression. When our eyes meet, I melt like butter on a biscuit.

"Well," I say, "now that she knows you're here, you may want to keep the fridge stocked with chicken."

He shakes his head and takes a deep breath. "I can't believe that happened. My heart is still racing."

"Welcome to Alabama!" I say, trying to lighten the

mood. He chuckles, that million-dollar Hollywood smile sending butterflies straight to my gut. "I really can't apologize enough."

"It's fine. Just do me a favor and warn the next guy who rents your house."

"I will."

Again we stand there, looking at each other for what seems like an age.

"Do you want some water or something? My assistant stocked the pantry for me. I'm not sure what all is in there, but you're welcome to anything."

"No, I should get back home. I have, um, laundry and stuff."

Laundry and stuff? Really? I am so lame.

"Okay."

But I don't leave. I just stand here. I think I'm in shock. He raises his eyebrows but I still don't move.

"Is the house okay?" I ask.

He grins and looks out over the property. "It's perfect. Better than I'd even imagined."

"Great! I'm glad you like it."

He nods. Again with the awkward silence.

"Alright, well, I'll let you get back to whatever you were doing. Are you able to get back in? I have the spare key if you need it."

"No, the front door is still unlocked. I need to remember about the back door next time."

"Great! Well, you have my number, so if you need anything else, call me."

"Thank you. I will."

I turn to walk back to my car. I want to run, but that seems a little dramatic.

"Kendall!" he calls from behind. The sound of my name coming from his mouth makes my heart stop. I turn and he's jogging towards me.

"Yes?" I say in a voice more high-pitched than I'd intended. When he approaches, I'm struck again by the fact that he's Pierre Chatham, of all people. I haven't been to the grocery store in ten years without seeing his face on some magazine cover at the register.

"I'd appreciate it if you didn't share what happened," he says. "I'm a little embarrassed, to be honest."

"Oh! Of course. I won't tell a soul." Except Patsy. I'm definitely telling Patsy.

"Please don't share my phone number either. I've had to change it so many times—it gets old."

"I totally get it. You can trust me."

"Thank you."

"If I don't see you again, good luck with your movie!"

He smiles and nods. I turn and walk to my car, knees shaking. When I get in to pull away, I look up to see him standing in the same spot. I wave, back out of the driveway, and leave. In my rearview mirror, he's standing by the road, watching my taillights.

*P*atsy will kill me if she finds out I kept this from her for more than five minutes, but I don't want to tell her over the phone. The first thing I do is go home and make myself look halfway decent with a shower, makeup, and real clothes.

Then I head to the baseball fields. I don't even have to ask where she is. With five boys, she always has at least one playing ball on a Saturday in early summer.

I park in the full lot and immediately see Patsy's middle son, Buck, running between the fences, his pants covered in red dirt. He sees me, stops what he's doing, and comes to give me a hug. I ask him where his mom is and he points me in the right direction.

The ball park is a diamond of four baseball fields with a concession stand in the middle. It's always crowded in the late spring and early summer. There's not much else going on in Magnolia Row on a Saturday afternoon.

I walk to the bleachers where Patsy is sitting on the top row. She's with her mother and has her youngest son, Hunter, on her lap. She waves when she sees me, but looks confused. I motion for her to come down, so she gives Hunter to her mom, then makes her way to where I'm waiting. In the background, a loud crack from a baseball bat startles me and the crowd begins to cheer.

"Kendall, what are you doing here?" Patsy asks. Today's look is what she calls "casual Patsy": Magnolia Row High t-shirt, cut-off shorts that show off her tone, tanned legs, and floral flip-flops.

"We need to go somewhere quiet." I grab her and pull her towards a picnic table at the edge of the park.

Her face drops. "Are you okay?"

"I'm fine, I promise. But I'm about to tell you something that you absolutely cannot tell anyone."

"Please tell me you finally killed F-er," she says with a too-big smile.

"No, I did not kill Tucker."

"Burned his house down?"

"No."

"Keyed his truck?"

"Patsy," I say, my tone curt.

She sighs. "Fine. A girl can dream."

"Of violence?"

"Only to those who deserve it."

We reach the table farthest from other people and sit down.

"You're not going to believe what happened this morning."

"Oh my god. Please tell me this is about the mystery man renting your house!"

I open my mouth, then pause. The words stick in my mouth as she raises her eyebrows in anticipation. It's like I don't even believe what happened a mere hour ago.

She grabs my hand. "Out with it! The suspense is killing me!"

"Okay. So, I met the person renting my house."

Her face lit up. "Is it someone famous?"

"Oh yeah. This must be a huge movie."

"Who is it?"

"You cannot tell a soul. Not even your mother."

"I promise, I promise!"

I look around to make sure we're still alone. "It's Pierre Chatham."

I swear she stops breathing for a solid thirty seconds.

"Pierre f-ing Chatham," she whispers.

"Yes."

"THE Pierre f-ing Chatham." This time she's a bit louder, so I gesture for her to lower her volume.

"Yes."

Then she squeals the loudest, highest pitch a human can make, eliciting stares from people walking nearby and a kid in the adjacent outfield.

"Ssssshhh! I told you to keep it quiet. You seriously cannot tell anyone. I can't have people showing up at the house and stalking him."

"I knew I should've put a camera in that house."

I simply shake my head at that comment. She's not joking.

"But I *love* him! He's hilarious in those movies he did with Sandra Bullock, where she's the mob boss and he's her oblivious boy toy."

"Didn't see them."

"And he was the soldier in that movie where he dies and the girl waiting for him back home thinks he'd forgotten about her, but then she gets the letters he'd been writing her like a year after the war's over. Oh my god, I bawled my eyes out. I think he was nominated for something for that movie."

"Didn't see it either."

"Go home and watch them! All of them! Everything he's in is good."

"That seems a little creepy now that I know him."

"You talked to him?"

"Oh yeah. We met."

Her mouth drops and it looks like her head is going to explode.

"In person?"

I nod, then proceed to tell her the whole story.

"Well, God bless Bertha!" she exclaims when I finish.

"No! I felt terrible. Half of our conversation was me apologizing." I shake my head.

"But if it weren't for that, we wouldn't know he's living there!"

"I wish I didn't know. It was so awkward. I was so awkward. Now he's going to go back to Hollywood and tell everyone about the strange little person he rented a house from in Alabama and her pet alligator."

She rolls her eyes. "No, he's not."

"I just hope if I see him again, I've at least brushed my hair."

Behind us, the loud crack of a baseball bat is followed by cheers and parents yelling. Patsy turns to look, checking on her free-range children.

"I hope you do see him again." she says, turning her attention back to me. "We can be friends with him!"

"He's not here to make friends. He's here to shoot a movie."

She crosses her arms and sighs. "Pierre f-ing Chatham."

I nod at her beaming face, then we mutually burst out laughing.

"Pierre f-ing Chatham," I say.

PIERRE

$\mathcal{I}$ didn't bring much on my trip from California, so it doesn't take long to get settled in the lake house. I can't get over how gorgeous this space is. It's comfortable without being ostentatious, low-key but quality. Exactly the vibe I need.

I even love the art in the house. There are exquisite photos of the river and even some of the local historic homes on the walls. They're all bright and happy, like if Mayberry were in color. It's clear whoever decorated has a good eye and a soft spot in their heart for this town.

Following Kendall's instructions, I go to the Piggly Wiggly right before they close and clean them out of rotisserie chickens. I'm sure everyone thinks I'm a creep, since I'm wearing a low baseball hat and sunglasses close to nine o'clock at night and carrying enough poultry to stock a KFC franchise, but no one seems to recognize me, so I let it go.

The next day I go through the movie script again, make

notes, and rehearse some lines in front of the bathroom mirror. I love this story, I love my character, and I love the crew I'll be working with. I even love this town.

I love everything except Marina Breton being my co-star. I'm finally at a point in my career where I'm getting serious roles, nominations, and my choice of scripts. I should be excited to do another drama, but Marina has cast a cloud of dread over this shoot already. Maybe I'm wrong and she's matured since the last time we worked together. Maybe.

One can hope.

After fretting over the movie all day, I relax on the deck with a book I can't focus on and a glass of merlot. It's a covered space with an overhead fan, citronella candles to deter mosquitoes, and a soft warm breeze blowing in from over the river. This time, I make sure I have the key to the back door in my pocket. The last thing I want is to have to call Kendall again.

She is cute, though. Awkward, yes, but in an endearing way. She's naturally beautiful, even though she looked like she'd just rolled out of bed when we met. But even that was adorable. And she had the sweetest smile. Genuine. Not like the women I usually meet, who immediately transform into contrived things to try to impress me. She didn't even ask for a photo or an autograph, which was nice.

Kendall is warm, and so…normal. It's refreshing, despite the bizarre circumstances of our meeting. And her Southern accent is so charming I could listen to her talk about nothing all day.

I sound like such a sap.

Maybe I do want to call her again, but this time not to be rescued from an alligator.

I take my wine glass and walk to the ledge of the porch. The moon is full and its reflection dances across the lazy roll of the river. I take in the pulsating sound of a symphony of insects from the nearby woods and, when I look up, I can actually see stars. I close my eyes and breathe.

This is peace. This is quiet.

This is the opposite of LA.

I wonder if Kendall likes living here, if this is her hometown, and what kind of house she lives in. If she has kids, a dog, hobbies. All I know about her is that she's an accountant with a nice rental property and does not wear a wedding ring.

I should call her.

No, I'm only here for a short time. What's the point? Meet a girl I actually like only to leave? What if she runs to the tabloids to sell our story? What if she posts crazy stuff about me online? Is it even worth it?

I take a long sip, finishing my wine, then look at my phone. Kendall's number is the first to pop up on my recent calls, but I scroll past and instead call Harriett.

"Bored yet?" she asks as soon as she answers. No *hello*, no *how are you*. Just straight to the point, which is why I love her.

I laugh. "No, actually. It's nice here. I kinda like it."

"Your movie set is my worst nightmare. That town is boring as shit."

"Turns out," I say, "not so boring after all." I proceed to

tell her about Kendall and the alligator. She listens intently with the occasional "no way" peppered through my story.

"Harriett, I can't stop thinking about her."

"Bertha the alligator?"

"No, Kendall."

"Really? She's cute and all, but not your type."

"Exactly!" I exclaim, raising an arm in excitement as if Harriett can actually see me. "She's normal! I get zero crazy vibes from her."

"Have you seen her today?"

"No, but I'm thinking about calling her."

"Okay," she says, sounding unsure. "Be careful. You're not some a random guy off the street."

"I know, I know."

We end the call and I sit back down in the rocking chair. I think on it a little more while taking sips of my wine.

I'll call Kendall tomorrow. I just need to come up with an excuse to talk to her again.

KENDALL

It's a slow Monday. May is always quiet; all I have to work on is payroll stuff for some local businesses. Patsy comes in with coffee, asks me if I've heard from Pierre (I haven't), puts her Taylor Swift playlist on our office Bluetooth speaker, and sits at the front desk to do her nails.

Then my cell phone rings.

No one ever calls me, so Patsy immediately turns the music down and runs to my open office door.

I look at the number. It's a California area code, so it has to be Pierre or his assistant. I didn't save either of their numbers and I'm not sure which one it is, but they're the only California people I know.

I look up at Patsy, wide-eyed.

"Answer it!" she says, impatient.

"Hello?" I answer, trying to sound natural but bordering on shrill.

"Hi, Kendall?"

Oh my god. It's Pierre. My heart stops.

"Pierre? Hi!"

Patsy starts jumping up and down and has to cover her own mouth to keep from screaming. I motion for her to get out of my office, but she shakes her head and tries to calm herself.

He clears his throat. "How are you?" he asks, sounding a little nervous, which is baffling.

"I'm okay. Is something wrong? I hope Bertha—"

"No, everything is great. I got the rotisserie chickens like you suggested."

"Great!"

Awkward silence. I rack my brain for something to say to him, but I come up blank. It's like my mind is completely erased every time I talk to him.

"Uh, listen," he says, "this may sound a little weird, but I have a favor to ask of you."

"Sure. How can I help?" Me? What could I possibly do for Pierre Chatham, of all people?

Besides, you know, save him from an alligator.

"Well, I've been working on my accent for this movie, and I think it would do me some good to be around some locals to get a feel for it."

"Um…okay?" I try not to sound confused.

"Is there a place where you guys like to hang out? Like a bar or restaurant or something?"

This is surreal. Anywhere I tell him to go is going to pale in comparison to places he's probably been to in fancy places like L.A., New York, and Europe.

"Most people go to Cattywampus," I say.

"Catty what?"

"Cattywampus. It's a brewery."

"Great! I love craft beer."

"Great!" Again, awkward silence. I have no idea what to say to this man.

"Where is it?"

Surely he has a phone to look this up. I'm completely bumfuzzled. "On the river, close to the bridge."

"Perfect! Are you free Wednesday night?"

I feel like I've been hit in the gut by a bowling ball of panic. "Wait. You want me to go with you?"

Patsy's mouth has hit the floor and her whole body is shaking. I put up my hand to shield my eyes and turn away.

"Of course! I'd feel weird going to a bar alone, and you're the only person I know in town."

I think I'm in shock. Is this a date, or does he want a random person to sit with? Doesn't he have other movie star friends coming to town? What could we possible have to talk about?

"Um, I don't know."

Patsy gives me a *what-is-your-problem* look.

"I don't mean to make it weird. You were very sweet the other day, and I wanted to get to know you a little better. If you have plans with your boyfriend or whomever—"

"No, no boyfriend. I'm sorry. I'm being rude. You caught me off guard is all."

"So is that a yes?"

Holy shit. I'm going out with Pierre Chatham. "Yes. I can meet you at 5:30?"

"Sounds great! See you then."

I hang up and Patsy squeals.

"Did I hear that right? Do you have a date with Pierre f-ing Chatham?"

"I don't know?" I know I look completely shell-shocked.

"You're meeting him for drinks?"

"Yes."

"Is anyone else going to be there?"

"I don't think so."

"That's a date!"

"I'm going to be sick," I say, putting my head down on my desk. I haven't been on a date since my divorce, nor do I have any plans to start dating anytime soon. The thought of getting close to someone, building this whole new life, then having it disappear out from under me again…it's too much.

"No, you're fine. You are going to rock this date and have the time of your f-ing life." Patsy walks around my desk and kneels beside my chair like she's comforting a child.

"What am I doing?" I ask her. "He's only in town for a few weeks. He's a movie star. Why would a movie star want me?"

"Because you're beautiful, Kendall! You deserve the hottest guy on the planet, and he just so happens to be living in your house!"

"This is such a bad idea. Where can this even go?"

"Nowhere! That's the point! He's the perfect rebound!"

"I feel like the statute of limitations on rebounds has expired. It's been three years."

She rolls her eyes. "Imagine what F-er would think if he found out you're dating Pierre Chatham."

I have to admit she has a point. Once I show up at Cattywampus with the Hollywood "it guy", the entire town will know within a day. Tucker's phone will explode.

So will his head.

"What if I like him? He's only here for two months, tops."

"Then you'll have a great story to tell your grandkids one day! Besides, you already said yes. You can't get out of it now."

"I can't believe this is happening."

"We only have two days to pick out your outfit. Let's go upstairs!"

*P*atsy vetoes everything in my chifforobe, which serves as my closet since the loft doesn't have one big enough for anything other than a mop and bucket.

I close the office early and we walk to Cotton Blossoms Boutique. Patsy picks out a strapless green and white gingham dress and white sandals. I used to wear clothes like this all the time, but they ended up in the Goodwill bag when I moved.

"You look amazing!" she says, staring at me in the circle of mirrors in the dressing room. "Like your old self." Patsy honestly looks like she is about to cry.

I don't know whether to be touched or annoyed. "My old self was a sap."

"Come on. This is the perfect outfit for your date."

I reluctantly agree, buy the dress and shoes, and go back to my loft, where I spend the rest of the evening with the remote and a bag of popcorn.

PIERRE

I get to Cattywampus Brewery early. It's in an old red brick cotton mill on the river with faded white lettering on the side. I park my rental car in the gravel parking lot, quickly glance around the spacious inside bar area to make sure Kendall hasn't arrived yet, then head to the back porch.

There aren't many people here, which I'm grateful for. The last thing I want is to be mobbed right when Kendall shows up.

The patio to the rear of the brewery is long, stretching the whole length of the place, and outfitted with rocking chairs and little wrought iron tables. I walk to the end and sit down in a creaky chair, taking comfort in the knocking sound as I settle into a rhythm.

This place is more peaceful than I could've imagined, though I shouldn't be surprised, given how idyllic the rest of the town looks. There's a long staircase going down to a massive dock with picnic tables at the water's edge. Somewhere close there's a barbeque grill going, sending the aroma of juicy pork to where I'm sitting. My stomach roars. I should've eaten before I came.

It's warm out, so I'm wearing a crisp white collared shirt with the top few buttons undone, khaki shorts, and boat shoes. As always, my baseball hat is pulled low and I don't remove my sunglasses.

I probably check my phone a hundred times before I catch movement out of the corner of my eye. Kendall walks onto the patio, looking amazing in the sweetest dress I've ever seen. Her long brown hair is down with loose, heavy curls at the ends, and though she's wearing make-up, it's minimal enough to not take away from how effortlessly stunning she is.

I stand up and take off my glasses so she'll see me. She walks with a short, quick stride, her hair bouncing over her bare shoulders.

"Hi! I hope you weren't waiting long."

"No, not at all. I'm always early."

"Okay."

We stare at each other. We've got to stop with this awkwardness. She's going to think I'm a moron. I've never been uncomfortable with women, but she makes me so nervous.

"Should we go in and get a drink?" I ask.

"Absolutely!" she says with a toothy, tight smile. I think she's as tense as I am.

When we walk in, the freezing air conditioning makes the skin on my arms prickle. Behind the bar, a weathered middle-aged lady takes our orders. She obviously recognizes me but doesn't make a big deal out of it, which I appreciate. She chats for a minute with Kendall and asks about her family while she pours our beer. Kendall gets the Pussycat Blonde and I get the Swamp Ass Stout. After we get our drinks, I open a tab and we settle at a table in the back corner of the room, where I face the wall so only Kendall can see me.

"I love the beer names," I say, grateful to have a conversation starter.

"Oh yeah!" she said, her face lighting up. "When they opened a few years ago, they did a whole contest in the weeks leading up to the grand opening. People came to get samples and cast ballots for names. If your idea won, you got a huge gift card. It was fun." She shrugs her shoulders. She seems giddy, though still a little uneasy.

"Sounds like a great idea. So, have you always lived here?" I ask.

She takes a sip of her beer and politely wipes her upper lip. "Yep. Born and raised. What about you? I guess you live in Hollywood or something?"

I laugh. "Bel Air."

"Wow. Sounds fancy. You must think we're a bunch of hicks."

"No, not at all! Apart from the whole alligator-trying-to-eat-me thing, I'm actually loving it so far." She giggles and my heart turns to putty. She's so sweet. It's refreshing. "It's quiet here," I continue. "I went to the grocery store without having to dodge photographers in the parking lot."

"For now. Once people find out you're in town, you can expect more attention. In fact," she pauses and motions towards the bar, "Calista has pointed you out to everyone who's ordered a drink."

"See," I say, "and they're not bothering me."

"Yet."

"Fans I can handle. Paparazzi, not so much. It's exhausting."

"Fair enough." We each take another sip of our beer. It's ice cold and delicious, some of the best craft beer I've ever had.

"So you're here for a movie?" she asks.

I nod.

"Tell me about it."

"It's a drama called *Gossamer Road*. It's set in a small Southern town, obviously. I play a single father who reunites with his high school sweetheart after she moves back to town. They pitched it as an updated *Hope Floats*, if you ever saw that. Except, in this one, the guy character is the one with the kid."

"I love *Hope Floats*! I bet it'll be great!"

"It should be. We have a good director and the script is strong. I'm excited to shoot here in Magnolia Row. It should make for a gorgeous film."

"Who else is in it?"

My stomach sinks. I don't even want to say her name. "Marina Breton is the female lead."

"Wow!" she says, her eyes wide. "Magnolia Row is not going to know what to do with all the star power."

I chuckle. "I hope we don't disrupt things too much. Movie productions tend to take over everything in a place this small."

Another awkward silence settles between us, and she fidgets with the condensation on her glass. "So…" she says, then bites her bottom lip. "Do you want me to help you rehearse or something?"

"No, I'm good. We have table reads next week."

She looks confused. "Oh. You'd said you wanted help with your accent. I'm not a dialect coach, but—"

I can't help but laugh at how naïve she is.

"What?" she asks with a confused little grin.

"I said that as an excuse to hang out with you."

She blushes, sits back in her chair, and gives me an uncomfortable, bewildered smile.

KENDALL

I clearly bumped my head and entered into some kind of twilight zone alternate universe. This really is a date.

"Why would you want to go out with me?" I blurt without thinking. I want to be charming, but I have no game. Like, at all.

He makes a face like he's taken aback.

"I'm sorry," I continue. "I mean, wouldn't you rather hang out with someone like Marina Breton?"

"Absolutely not." He shakes his head and laughs.

"But she's perfect. I'm just...I don't know."

"Marina is crazy. There's not a nice way to put it. I worked with her before and to say she was difficult is an understatement. She's fake, self-absorbed, and obsessed with her image and career. I'd much rather hang out with you. You're everything she's not."

I blush. "I'm sorry," I say again. "I'm not good with compliments."

"And you apologize too much."

"Oh. I didn't realize. I'm so—" He laughs as I catch myself. "You're right."

We each take another sip of our beer. I'm not normally a big drinker, but I'm taking gulps for the liquid courage. The after-work crowd is slowly trickling in, and people are staring at us as murmurs fill the room about the movie star in the back corner.

"Have you always lived in Bel Air?" I ask him.

"No. I grew up in LA, but it wasn't close to Bel Air by any means. I had a single mom. She was a teacher, so she had a decent job, but we still struggled. We lived in an apartment in a sketchy neighborhood."

I nod, picking at my nails under the table. I'm trying to act normal but I'm too nervous. "Is Pierre your real name? It sounds very French for a boy from Cali." Now all I can think about is how he said Marina Breton is contrived, and I can't help but feel like my tone has an artificial lilt. I keep telling myself to act normal, but I'm not sure I know how.

"No," he says. "My mom was a total Francophile. She was a French teacher, actually. Our whole apartment was covered in cheap Eiffel Tower art she'd find at flea markets and craft stores. She came with me to the Cannes Film Festival the year before she died, and afterwards I took her to Paris for a week. It was her only trip to France and ended up being the best vacation of my life."

His eyes mist as he clears his throat and looks out the windows towards the river. My heart melts. I'm surprised by how open he is. When we were married, Tucker was a closed book, his emotions locked in a safe, no key, at the bottom of the ocean. In fact, I don't know any guys who are this transparent. Everything he's thinking and feeling is written all over his face. It's refreshing.

"I'm sorry," I say.

"There you go apologizing again."

I half-laugh, half-sigh. "No, I mean about your mom."

"Thank you. I miss her."

He puts his drink down and leans back in his chair. I feel like I should change the subject. Dead mother is heavy topic for a first date—if this is a date. I'm still not entirely sure what's happening right now.

"How did you get your start acting?" I twirl my glass nervously on the table, then catch myself and stop. I hate that I'm this fidgety.

"I was outgoing and everyone thought I was a cute kid, so Mom got me an agent and pushed me into it early on. I've been stuck ever since."

I'm surprised by choice of words. He's living a life most people would kill for. "Stuck? You don't like it?"

"I like the craft," he says, his eyes narrowing at the word *craft*. "I don't like being a celebrity."

"If you weren't an actor, what would you do?"

He lifts his eyebrows. "Write a novel. Build furniture. Run an animal rescue. There are a lot of other things I could do. I'd like to just *be* for a while." He takes another sip of his drink and looks off into space for second. "I do love dogs, though. That's the first thing I'd do if I quit acting. If I had a whole pack of them running around my house, I'd be perfectly happy."

"Do you have one now?"

"No, I'm too busy bouncing from project to project. It would end up being my assistant's dog, and she's a cat person."

I'm picturing him rolling around in a field of wildflowers with about six golden retrievers and it's the most adorable image. I sigh.

"If you hate it so much, why don't you quit?" I ask.

"You mean get out of acting?" He kind of chuckles like I've lost my mind.

"Sure! It's been done. Didn't Doris Day do exactly the same thing? Quit Hollywood to rescue animals? Taylor Swift has a song about it."

"I think she did, actually. It's tempting. It's just not easy when acting is all I've ever known. All of my friends are in the industry. I'm at the height of my career. Besides, if I changed my mind after the fact, I'd be screwed. Once you leave, it's hard to break back in. People would think I'm nuts."

"Maybe they'd be jealous." I attempt a flirty tone, but I'm pretty sure I sound ridiculous.

He laughs. "Yeah, maybe." He fingers his glass, wiping the sweat from the sides. "What about you? What's your life story?"

I squirm in my seat. My life story is a failed marriage and a sad existence in a studio apartment watching murder shows. I'm not sure how to answer this question without killing the mood.

Then, as if on cue, I look up and see Tucker. He's glaring right at me. I feel the blood drain from my face and my stomach ties itself in knots. I think I'm going to puke.

Pierre puts his hand on mine. "Are you okay?" he asks.

I snap out of it, realizing I had gone silent long enough to make it weird. "I'm sorry," I said.

"Again with the apologies." He smiles and it makes me laugh.

Well, if Pierre can be transparent with his wounds, I guess I can too. "You want to know my story? He just walked in."

Pierre turns around and sees Tucker, who is standing behind a high-top table, completely unashamed of the fact that he's staring at us with confusion and shock. No doubt Calista told him who my mystery man is as soon as he walked up to the bar. Part of me wants to run away. The other part is smug. I'm here with Pierre f-ing Chatham, as Patsy would say.

"The guy with the Dave Matthews shirt?" he asks.

"Yep. That's my ex-husband."

Pierre turns again as Whitney approaches Tucker and puts her arms around him. He nods in our direction and she sees me at the table with Pierre. If it weren't for her cheap spray tan, the color would be draining from her face.

"And that's the girl he left me for."

Pierre smirks and looks back to me. "That guy? Really?" He shakes his head. "That's a guy who peaked in high school and that girl reeks of desperation."

I laugh. He's right. Tucker has definitely seen better days. He's weathered, and not in a sexy way. While he's not overweight, he somehow looks bloated all the time. As far as Whitney is concerned... yeah. Pierre is right. Fake lashes, fake boobs, hair extensions, acrylic nails. The only thing real on her is the massive diamond on her left hand.

"Any guy who will go for a girl like that doesn't deserve you."

Pierre and I lock eyes for a long moment. For the first time in years, or maybe ever, I feel seen. Really, truly, honestly seen in a way that makes me excited and nervous. Like his eyes reach into my soul and strip me of my armor. I've known him for three days and it suddenly feels like a lifetime. I shudder and snap myself out of it.

"Well, it's over now," I say quietly, then clear my throat.

"Glad to hear it."

I take another long sip of beer to finish it off.

"Another?" Pierre asks.

I nod.

When he gets up, I take the opportunity to truly absorb how dreamy he is. His hair is perfectly tousled, like he cares but not too much. He has olive skin that sets off eyes the color of the Gulf of Mexico. He looks like he stepped out of old Hollywood. It's easy to understand why he's a movie star. He's almost too perfect.

Before he can get to the bar, he's stopped by some girls who want selfies. He gracefully obliges, then gets our beer from Calista. Tucker and Whitney look incessantly from Pierre to me and back again, and though I try to ignore it, I really want to laugh.

Patsy would be loving this if she was here now.

PIERRE

I return to the table with our beer, feeling the heat of Kendall's nemeses' eyes on my back. If looks could kill, I'd be a dead man.

Kendall has her legs crossed, one white sandal dangling off her toes. It's so sexy I have to look away, fighting the urge to do something cheesy like kneeling to place it back on her foot.

I'm ridiculous.

I sit down and take a sip of my drink. "So apart from being divorced from the douchebag over there, what's your story?"

She blushes again. "I'm boring, actually."

"I don't believe that for a minute."

"No, really. That's one of the reasons Tucker gave for cheating on me. He said I was boring." There's an edge to her voice—she's still angry. Honestly, she probably has a right to be. If I could get away with walking over and

48

punching that guy in the face, I'd do it in a heartbeat just on principle.

"Let's not talk about him anymore," I say in an attempt to lift the mood. "Tell me your story. About your family, friends, hobbies, how you became an accountant with a stunning rental house on the lake."

"It is a fabulous house, isn't it?"

"I could stay there forever. I absolutely love it."

She looks down at her hands and picks at one of her nails. I've clearly hit a nerve.

"My dad was an accountant," she says. "He retired a few years ago, so I took over his practice and my parents moved to the beach. I'm an only child. I had a pretty typical, happy childhood. That's about it. See? Boring." She shrugs.

I shake my head. "Not boring. Happy childhoods aren't typical in my experience. You're very lucky. And rare."

"So you're a cynic?"

"Just a little."

"I guess I am lucky. We were pretty happy. Family dinners, church on Sunday, Mom and Dad loved each other. Blissfully boring. How's that?"

"Blissfully boring is good," I say, my eyes locked on hers. "Did you always want to be an accountant?"

"Lord, no," she says, wiping a little beer foam from her upper lip. "When I was little, I wanted to be a gymnast, but I was terrible. I was always hurting myself. Then I got into photography and I loved that, but the only way to make money in that field is to do weddings and family portraits, which would stress me out and take the joy out of the art. Accounting was much safer and practical, so photography became a hobby. I went to college not far from here, then came home and married Tucker. We were high school sweethearts, did the long-distance thing in college since he stayed here. After I graduated, we got married, built that beautiful dream house on the lake, and planned to have a bunch of kids. Then it all fell apart."

"And now?"

"Now? There's not much to say for now. I work. My best friend Patsy is my secretary, which makes the days fun and interesting. I live in a loft above my office. When I took over my dad's practice, it was filled with decades of old files, so I put all that in storage and turned the space into a little apartment for myself. It's small, but nice." She looks sad, maybe even a little embarrassed.

"You don't miss the house?"

She shakes her head defiantly. "I can't go back there."

I nod, then change the subject. "What about the photography? Do you still take pictures?"

"It's been years since I even took my camera out of the bag."

"Don't you miss it?"

"I don't really think about it, to be honest. But yeah, now that you mention it, I guess I do." Her voice has a sad, melancholic tone.

"What kind of photos did you take?"

"Nature stuff and local sites around town. I do have a pretty awesome picture of Bertha. I'll have to make you a copy before you go back to California."

I make a face, like a faux grimace. Then it dawns on me that she's probably the one who took the photos in the house, so I ask.

"Yep!" she says, looking a little sad. "Those are mine."

"They're amazing! You should get back into it."

"I might. I stay busy with work and everything, so it's hard." A shadow falls over her face.

"Are you happy?" The words come out of my mouth before I pause to ask if that was too forward. She squirms in her chair and looks down, so I know I've made her uncomfortable.

"I just am," she says. "I'm not really happy or sad. I guess I float along in a state of numb resignation." She raises her eyebrows and takes a deep breath. I think she's surprised herself with her own candor.

"You're not still pining for that guy over there, are you?" I motion over my shoulder to where I know he's still keeping an eye on us.

"Oh God, no. I could never trust him again. Patsy would kill me."

"That's a good friend."

"She is." Her face softens.

"It sounds like you're in a rut."

She nods.

"We can change that."

"Oh, can we now?" Her energy shifts back to being sweet and cheery and she chuckles. "Patsy is going to love you. She was ecstatic that I was hanging out with you today. She's the one who picked out this dress, actually."

"I love it. When we meet, I'll have to thank her."

She blushes again and tucks a strand of hair behind her ear. We stare at one another for a moment before two girls approach the table.

"Hi, Kendall!" They address her but look straight at me.

"Oh, hi," Kendall says, sitting up and looking slightly uncomfortable. She gives me a tense look.

"Hi, I'm Pi-" I begin before they cut me off.

"We know!" They sit down, uninvited, telling me how much they love my movies and asking what other celebrities are in town. I try to keep my answers short and to the point, but they aren't taking the hint. Kendall takes the opportunity for a restroom break, but when she gets back, the two girls are still there, not so much talking to me as talking at me. Kendall smiles at them when she approaches the table, but doesn't sit down.

"Pierre, maybe we should—" She gestures towards the door.

"Right!" I stand, taking the hint. "It was nice to meet you ladies." They ask for a selfie, which I oblige. Kendall walks away, waiting for me by the door while I close the tab. The entire time I'm standing at the bar, I can see her ex looking at me—along with everyone else in the place.

When we leave, Kendall opens the door before I have a chance to get it for her. She points to where she's parked and I follow. I place my hand on the small of her back and feel her body tense, though she doesn't say anything. Once we get to her car, she stops and turns to me.

"Thank you for inviting me out," she says. The soft light of the setting sun makes her glow, and I wish there was a way I could capture this without ruining the moment.

"We'll have to do it again," I say. "It sounds like you need to get out more."

"I apologize for everyone staring at you, and for those two girls who came to the table. I would've introduced you, but I could not remember their names for the life of me. I think one of them hooked up with Patsy's little brother under the bleachers during a Homecoming game my senior year."

I make a face and she shrugs.

"It's a small town. No one has secrets. Also, we're not used to having celebrities in Magnolia Row, so you might get more of those encounters while you're here."

"It's fine. By the way, you really need to get better at not apologizing. You have nothing to be sorry for."

She laughs. "I'll work on it."

"Listen, I have kind of a packed schedule with table reads over the next few days, then we start shooting. But I would like to see you again."

"Oh! Um—" She sounds surprised. Why would she be surprised? "Yeah, I guess that would be okay."

"Great! I'll be in touch once I get a better idea of my schedule."

"Sounds good!"

The familiar awkward silence settles between us again. The sun is beginning to set and casts long shadows from the pine trees on the edge of the property. Kendall doesn't break my gaze, so I lean in to give her a kiss before we leave. As soon as my mouth is less than an inch from hers, she gasps and takes a step back, nearly losing her balance in the gravel. I grab her arm to catch her.

"I, uh, I—" Her face turns bright red. "I want to apologize, but you keep getting on to me about it." We both laugh.

"Don't apologize. I'm the one who is sorry. I shouldn't have assumed it was okay. I enjoyed talking to you tonight, and you looked radiant. I just...I don't know. I thought it was okay."

"No, it—it is. I mean, I'm not." She's flustered, and I feel terrible. She takes a deep breath. "It's not you. You're wonderful. In fact, you're perfect, as far as I can tell. It's me. I wasn't expecting...well, I don't really know what I was expecting. Ugh. I hate myself. This is awkward."

I reach out and rub my hand on her arm. "It's fine. Really. And don't say you hate yourself. It's bad for your energy."

Her face softens. This has to be the first time she's been on a date since her divorce. Part of me sees red flags but, at the same time, it's refreshing to see a woman with her heart on her sleeve. It's also nice to talk to someone who isn't trying to be some artificial version of themselves that they think will attract a celebrity. She's genuine.

"Look," I say, brushing my fingers across her hand, "take a few days. I'll get in touch with you and if you want to hang out again, great. If not, thank you for a wonderful evening. I'm delighted I got to meet you. No pressure for future dates."

She nods and relaxes. "That sounds good. Thank you." She squeezes my hand, then immediately releases it to wrap her arms around me in a hug. I hesitate for a beat, then lean down to return the gesture. She's tiny in my arms and I feel like if I hug too tight, she'll break.

When she pulls away, I open her door and she gets in. Keys in hand, she waves at me. I return the gesture and close the door, then walk to my rental car to begin the short drive to the lake house.

KENDALL

I drive the three blocks it takes to get back to my office/apartment. I could've walked but these shoes hurt my feet and I didn't want to be limping on my date.

Yes, that was actually a date.

I'm still in shock.

And Tucker was there. I'm not sure how I feel about that. Part of me wants to laugh my tail off, but part of me doesn't want to think of him at all. I don't want to be smug; I want to be indifferent. I want him to not exist in this town so I can live my life without the cloud of that relationship hanging over me.

I walk up the narrow, uneven steps to my apartment. This building is over eighty years old and the wood creaks under my feet. The paint is peeling from the plaster walls, which makes it look a little haunted. Patsy keeps trying to talk me into some funky floral wallpaper and extra lighting, but I haven't gotten around to it. She is right, though. It really would brighten things up.

I collapse on my bed, my head still spinning. Pierre Chatham likes me.

Me.

Little nobody me.

Pierre f-ing Chatham.

The bad thing is, I like him too. He's so open, so matter-of-fact, so attentive. I don't feel like I have to try hard to keep his attention the way I always did with Tucker. Pierre is down-to-earth. He's polite and not at all pretentious about being famous. On top of all that, he has that irresistible Hollywood hunk look that makes me want to internally combust.

I pull my phone from my purse and text Pierre to let him know I got home okay. A few minutes later, it dings in return, letting me know he made it home—to my old home—as well. He tells me he hopes I have a good night, but I don't respond.

I can't let this go on. I'm already smitten, but the thought of losing my heart again makes me physically ill. As soon as I let down my guard and see him again, I know I'll fall harder, and it'll be that much worse when he leaves in a few weeks.

I cannot go through that again. The divorce nearly killed me. It's not worth the risk. But damn if he isn't tempting.

57

he next day my mom calls me at exactly eight in the morning, right as I'm unlocking the front door to my office.

"What's this I hear about you dating a movie star?"

"How did you—"

"Calista saw you and texted your dad."

I roll my eyes. "Dear lord."

"So? How in the world did you end up on a date with Pierre Chatham at Cattywampus?"

I tell her the short version and we end the call with my promise to keep her updated, but the last thing I want is my parents involved in my love life. After the whole Tucker debacle, they're understandably a little overprotective. The less they know, the better.

Patsy arrives earlier than usual, throws her purse on the front desk, and comes straight into my office without so much as a good morning.

"So?" she asks, her hands shaking with excitement.

"What?"

"You know what. How was the date?"

I sigh and lean back in my chair, closing my eyes and putting my hands on my head.

"He's perfect."

Patsy squeals. "I knew it! I need all the details. This is the best thing that could've happened to you!"

"No, Patsy. It's not."

"Why? What happened? You said he's perfect."

"It's not him; it's me. I'm very much not perfect."

"Oh, don't start with that crap again. You need to move on and a big celebrity is the perfect guy to get you out of your head." She sits down in the chair in front of my desk. "Tell me every detail from the beginning. I already know Tucker was there."

"What? How?"

"Mercuria Beaumont texted me."

I roll my eyes. This town.

I go through our date, line by line from what I can remember. When I tell her about the botched kiss at the end of the night, I thought her eyes were going to pop out of her head like a cartoon.

"Shut the f-ing door. Pierre f-ing Chatham tried to kiss you and you turned away from him?"

I nod, giving her a tense, toothy smile.

"We need to take you in for a lobotomy or something. When Pierre Chatham kisses you, you're supposed to kiss him back!" She looks at me like I've grown a third eye.

"No. This is bad! All bad! Nothing good can come from this. There's no way I'll come out of this without getting hurt."

"You don't know that."

"I do. I felt crazy close to him yesterday. We talked about his past, my past. He has this way of seeing into my soul. It's unnerving and incredibly sexy at the same time. If this goes any further, I'm going to fall so hard that the splat will leave a permanent mark and you will never be able to clean it up."

She shakes her head. "Like Humpty Dumpty?"

"Yes! Exactly. Think of me as an egg on a ledge."

Patsy's expression softens. She walks around my desk, kneels, and takes my hand.

"Kendall," she says, "it's not a bad thing to be scared. I know the divorce was hard, but—"

"No," I say, pulling away from her, and a dam inside of me breaks. "You don't know. You and Garion are perfect. You got your happily ever after with your high school sweetheart. You have no idea what it's like for that to blow up in your face. I hope you never do."

She takes a deep breath. "You deserve to be happy, and you're not happy holed up in your apartment all the time. You never will be at this rate. Put yourself out there. You never know…"

"This isn't a practical dream to chase. He's from a completely different world."

"He's not an alien."

"He might as well be."

"For all we know, he could sweep you off your feet and whisk you away to California to live a life of luxury."

"Not only is that highly unlikely, it's not even what I would want. This whole thing is an exercise in futility."

"It could work out! Crazier things have happened. If it doesn't, who cares? You'll be one step closer to moving on."

"You've watched way too many princess movies."

"That's not the point." She raises her eyebrows and gives me her stern mom look. "Consider it. When he calls—"

"*If* he calls."

"No, we're sending good vibes out into the universe. Manifesting. When he calls, give him a chance."

I lean forward, gaze at the spreadsheets on my computer screen, and tap my pencil on the desk. Patsy stands up and glares at me, hands on hips.

I sigh. "I'll think about it."

PIERRE

I decide to leave Kendall alone the day after our date. She didn't say anything after I texted her to have a good night, so I assume she needs time to process.

I hope that's all it is, anyway.

Ever since that night, I can't help but feel like I'm living in the ruins of her past life. Despite the gorgeous photography and artful touches here and there, I also note a few empty nails and blank surfaces where I imagine wedding and vacation photos were once displayed. It suddenly feels sterile and cold.

Standing in the kitchen, I envision Kendall beside me cooking or walking down the hall in a bathrobe and slippers. I picture her on the back porch with me or watching a movie together in the living room. I think of all these little scenarios and the house feels warm again, especially when I imagine her lying beside me in bed.

The bed she once shared with someone else.

It's a strange feeling to occupy the broken dreams of the girl you like. I'm not sure how to feel about it.

I spend the day trying not to think about Kendall and going over the script again. I even have a video chat with my dialect coach in LA. Later, I have another glass of wine on the back deck of the house, and this time I'm prepared when Bertha comes crawling into the yard for her evening snack. Watching her waddle back to the river with a rotisserie chicken in her mouth, I shake my head in disbelief. This is my life for the next several weeks.

My phone has been buzzing since midday with calls from Marina, which I ignore. She must've arrived in Magnolia Row. After five ignored calls and three unanswered texts, I ring Harriett to tell her about my date with Kendall.

"Sounds like she has issues," Harriett says bluntly.

"I don't think she's dated since her divorce."

"Yeah, and it sounds like she's not crazy about the attention you bring either."

"No, she's not." She has a point.

"Which is part of the appeal for you, I'm sure." Another good point.

"You're right. I can't tell you the last time I had a date with a regular person. It's refreshing."

"I take it you are not going to cave in to the studio and let those Marina dating rumors fly?"

"Nope. I refuse to participate in that whole charade. It encapsulates everything I hate about Hollywood. It's asinine. I shouldn't have to do that to make art."

"Good luck telling that to the rest of the industry. Let

me know how everything turns out with Kendall. I have to run. There's a party in Topanga Canyon tonight."

"I will. Have fun."

I hang up the phone, refreshed and a little buzzed from the wine. The wind picks up and rustles through the trees. I find myself wishing I had a hammock so I could stay out here all night. Instead, I go back inside and crawl into bed in my boxers. The sheets are soft against my skin and I imagine what it would be like for Kendall to be lying beside me. I close my eyes and drift off to sleep.

The next day, I wake up in a great mood. Since I've been in Magnolia Row, I don't dread getting up every day. I shower, eat a snack for breakfast, check my email and go over the shooting schedule, then drive into town to see if I can pry Kendall away from her office for lunch.

Once I get to Main Street, parking is somewhat of an issue. The film crew is already setting up and a lot of the street parking is blocked off. Locals have gathered on the sidewalk to watch, and I recognize the two girls from Cattywampus standing in front of Kendall's office. I roll my eyes. They're probably staking out the place, looking for me.

Unable to find parking, I turn off into a relatively empty church parking lot. I get out, pull my hat low, and look down as I walk so hopefully no one will recognize me.

I make it to Kendall's office door when I hear the girls from the bar call my name. I give them a short wave, then duck into the office as quickly as I can.

The space is a decent size and nicely decorated. The walls are white and there are historic photos from the town blown up and displayed in heavy frames. I assume these were also taken by Kendall, as they have the same aesthetic and deep angles. There's one desk in the front with a door behind it, which I assume leads back to Kendall's office.

A short blonde pokes her head out of the back office. Her face lights up when she sees me.

"Oh my God! You're Pierre Chatham!" She turns around. "Kendall, it's Pierre!"

"Hi," I say as the girl runs to me and gives me a big hug, as if I am an old friend she hasn't seen in ages.

"I'm Patsy," she says.

"Like Patsy Cline," I say, as if I hadn't known who she was before she said her name.

She laughs, almost maniacally. "Yep! My mama named me after her. Imagine her disappointment when I couldn't carry a tune in a bucket." She's charming, if a little nuts.

"Is Kendall—"

"She's back here." Patsy grabs my arm and drags me to the office, where Kendall is staring into a compact and frantically wiping her mouth with a napkin. She's wearing a simple button-down shirt with khakis, her hair in a ponytail. On her desk are two full sandwiches.

"Pierre! I had no idea you were coming today."

"It was a spur of the moment decision. I hope that's okay."

"It's perfectly fine!" replies Patsy.

Kendall gives her a piercing look, which Patsy completely ignores.

"I was going to ask you to lunch, but it looks like you're already eating."

"No, we've barely had a bite! She can go to lunch with you." Patsy grabs Kendall's sandwich and throws it in a small trash can. Kendall cuts her a sharp look.

"Is that okay?" I ask Kendall.

"Sure," she says. "Let me grab my purse."

Patsy, grinning and biting her bottom lip, steps aside so Kendall and I can get out of the office.

"Have fun, you two!" she calls.

Kendall shakes her head, and together we walk out into the bright Alabama sun.

KENDALL

I could murder Patsy right now. Yes, I probably would've gone to lunch with Pierre anyway, but still. I don't like being put on the spot.

"What's good around here?" asked Pierre as soon as we're out on the sidewalk. "Do you want another sandwich?"

"Sure," I say, dodging people on the sidewalk who have turned to look at us. "Bread Crumbs is a few doors down. They're the best—and only—sandwiches in town."

"Great!" he says, putting a hand on my back the way he did the night of our date. I try to not freak out, but he must feel me tense up because he pulls back, though he says nothing.

When we walk into Bread Crumbs, everyone turns around and stares, especially after Pierre removes his sunglasses. I recognize most of the folks here, though there are a few tables full of people who are likely film crew and not locals. It is much more crowded than usual.

"Do you want to get it to go?" I ask. Pierre is looking at the menu on the wall, completely ignoring the fact that we're the center of attention.

"I'm with you," he says. "I'm down for whatever."

We order sandwiches. I get my usual tomato turkey and he orders a fried green tomato BLT. Curran Briddell, the girl working behind the counter, has a bright pink pixie cut and massive blue doe eyes. She looks from me to Pierre, obviously trying to figure out what's going on.

"Kendall, I didn't know you were friends with a movie star," she says, eyeing Pierre like she's hungry.

"He's just renting my house," I answer. "I'm showing him around town."

"Is it true the movie is looking for extras?" she asks, directing her question to Pierre. "I was in all the plays in high school. I'd love to—"

"I don't really get involved in that," he says. "If they start looking, I'm sure they'll put out a call in the paper or on social media."

She leans over the counter, obviously trying to show her cleavage to Pierre, only to be disappointed when he pulls out his phone and begins scrolling instead. She stands up and glares at me as we hear "order up!" called from the kitchen.

"Thank you, Curran," I say as she hands us our bagged lunch.

"Mmhm." She smirks.

"Do you want to go back to your office?" Pierre asks when we're back out on the sidewalk.

"No. Patsy won't leave us alone."

He laughs. "Yeah, she was something else."

"I apologize for her earlier. She was a little too excited to meet you."

Pierre stops in his tracks and takes my hand, sending shivers through my whole body. "Kendall," he begins. I swear my heart stops when he says my name. "Stop apologizing for everything."

I grin. "You're right. I know you're right. Bad habit. I'll work on it."

"Where do you want to eat?"

"There's a little park by the river with picnic tables. It's close to Cattywampus."

"Perfect."

We walk in silence and he doesn't try to put his hand on my lower back again, though I find myself wanting him to. I'm so wishy-washy I'm annoying myself. If there were a title for sending mixed signals, I'd be the queen.

We get to the park and find a table under the shade of an oak tree. Spanish moss hangs low and sways in the warm, gentle breeze coming off the river.

"God, it's beautiful here," Pierre comments.

"It is," I say, looking out across the horizon. "Though sometimes I forget."

"Thank you for coming to lunch with me," he says as he unwraps his sandwich. "I hope it's okay that I surprised you."

"Yeah, it's fine. I wasn't sure if you'd really reach out again after the way I ended things the other night...which I am not going to apologize for."

"Good," he says with a mouth full of food. Then he

chuckles and wipes his mouth. "This sandwich is amazing! I've never had fried green tomatoes, and now I don't know how I lived without them. What is that sauce?"

"Remoulade. You'll have to get your fill of Southern food while you're here."

"I definitely will. I keep smelling barbeque."

"Yep! Patsy's brother-in-law owns the barbeque joint. It's good. There's also an amazing soul food joint. We have one nice-ish dine-in with Cajun food and a seafood place on the river south of town. Oh, and a catfish food truck."

"I'm in trouble! If I gain thirty pounds in the next few weeks, the wardrobe people will kill me." He wipes his mouth and takes a huge gulp of water.

"When do you start filming?"

"We have table reads tomorrow, then shooting begins next week."

"Are the other actors in town yet?"

Out of the corner of my eye, I see a gaggle of girls looking at us through their phones, most likely taking pictures of Pierre to post on social media. If Pierre notices, he ignores them.

"I think Marina is. She's been calling."

"You didn't answer?"

"Nope."

"How are you going to work with her if you can't stand to talk to her?"

"Let's just say I'll deserve the Oscar for this performance."

"You were nominated once before, weren't you?"

"Twice, actually. It's a surreal experience. By the time

the awards season rolls around, you're more than a year removed from the project and you've moved on to other things. Then you're there with all these people you've looked up to your whole life. The cameras are in your face. It's like an out-of-body thing. I can't describe it."

"Well, on TV it looks magical."

He laughs. "That's Hollywood!" He finishes his sandwich and balls up the wrapper. "I guess it is magical in retrospect. In the moment, it's incredibly tense. You have to be removed from it to appreciate it. I know a few people who've won those big awards, and they say they don't even remember the ceremony. It's like your body goes into shock, then the next morning you wake up and there's a little gold man on your nightstand."

"Do you want to win one?"

He makes a face and tilts his head slightly. "I used to. I'd be grateful if I did, but I don't really focus on it as much, especially since my mom died. It's like I wanted it for her."

"What do you want for you?"

He pauses and stares at me for a long minute. "I think I could ask you the same thing."

I freeze. Like he did Wednesday evening, he gives me the look, the one that penetrates my being.

"What do you mean?" I ask with trepidation.

"I had an epiphany," he says, tilting his head.

"About me?"

"About us."

"Us? We're an us now?" My stomach knots, but I maintain my composure.

"I know why I'm so drawn to you, apart from the obvious."

"The obvious?"

"Yeah. You're gorgeous, sweet, down-to-earth. There's a whole host of adjectives I could use to describe you. That's the obvious."

I feel blood rush to my face and I know I'm beet red. I laugh nervously and look down to pick at my almost-finished sandwich. "Um, thank you?"

"Still struggling with the compliments?"

"Yes. Very much so."

"You'll have to get used to them. You deserve to hear them every day."

"I'll work on it." We pause and I take a sip of water. "What is your epiphany, then?"

"My epiphany is that I'm drawn to you because we've both spent our lives living for other people. Now that those people are no longer in our lives—from death or divorce or what have you—we find ourselves…" He pauses and looks out to the horizon. "…unmoored."

"Unmoored." I nod and think about this. He has a point. "Good word. You should try your hand at writing."

"It's on the old bucket list."

I finish the last bite of my lunch, fold the wrapper, put it in the bag on the table, then take a long drink of water.

"Maybe you're right," I concede. Something about his words bring my walls down a notch, enough to admit to myself that I am, in fact, unmoored.

"So, what do you want for you?" he says, tilting his head to the side.

"I asked you first," I answer, deflecting.

"Fair enough. If I'm being honest with myself, I want to leave Hollywood. Leave the pressure. Leave the circus. Maybe do a few indie pictures every now and then, but mostly I want to be left alone."

"Do you want a family?" I ask.

"With the right person, in the right place, absolutely. Not in LA. Or New York, for that matter. Maybe Ireland. It's nice there. Or Maine. Right now, I have no one and where I end up depends on who I'm with, which is the most important factor. It would be nice to have that anchor. That stable foundation."

"Yeah." He's right. We are the same.

This is torture.

"What about you?" he asks.

I sigh, knowing I may as well be honest. "I want kids. I want someone to build my life around. I want to get old and have a brood of grandbabies to feed. I thought I'd have that with Tucker but, in retrospect, it's for the best. He was never the right guy. I was trying to make him into something he's not. We were bad for each other."

I close my eyes after I finish talking. It's remarkable. I feel physically lighter, having admitted all of that. Simply saying the words lightens the load. Panic fills my core from the sudden unexpected honesty with him and myself, but I know it's a good thing. I need to open back up again.

My eyes water and I look at Pierre, whose expression mirrors my own. He reaches for my hand and I let him squeeze it. I rub my thumb across his smooth skin, then the familiar voice in my heart screams "no, no, no."

I let go of his hand, close my eyes, and shake my head. "I can't get close to you like this. What are we doing? You live in California. It's practically a different world. If you're looking for a hook-up girl while you're here, you need to find someone else."

I stand up and grab our bag of trash, embarrassed that I basically word vomited all over him. He didn't deserve that. I'd panicked.

He also rises, then takes the bag from me.

"Here's the thing, Kendall. I'm not looking for a cheap thrill. I can't promise we're going to get married and live happily ever after. We just met. But I can tell you I have nothing but good intentions. I don't know what I'm doing. I don't know where this could lead, but I like you. I feel a strong pull to you that I haven't felt in years, if ever. I'm not ready to throw that away because of geography. Let's relax and see where this goes."

I look up at him. His brow has broken out with a small layer of sweat from the high sun, and his gaze holds so much sincerity that I feel the wall around my soul go down a little bit more.

"Okay," I say, my heart skipping a nervous beat.

He smiles and takes me in his arms. He's hot, literally, but I don't care.

When we release each other, he throws away our sandwich bags and we both realize that more people have gathered around the park watching us, some not even trying to hide that they're taking pictures.

"I don't know how you live like this," I say with a nod towards them.

"It wears on you, that's for sure," he replies as we begin the walk towards my office. "When can I see you again?" he asks.

"You're the one with the busy schedule. You tell me."

"Table reads are tomorrow, but we should be done in the afternoon. Do you want to come over for dinner? I'll cook for you."

"No, I'm not comfortable—"

"Oh, the house. Right."

"Yeah. I'm sorry. It's…bad memories and all."

"I get that. I can come to your place. Or we can go out, but that won't be very private."

"I don't know. I have a tiny kitchen."

"I can work with any kitchen. How is seven o'clock? Are you okay with a late dinner?"

"Yep."

"Is there anything in particular you want, or is there something you don't like?"

"I'm good with whatever. Surprise me."

We reach my office door and Patsy is craning over the computer to see how things are going. I turn to Pierre and point towards the exterior door adjacent to my office.

"Just ring the doorbell over there. There's a little staircase inside that goes up to my loft."

"Will do."

It gets awkward again. I want him to kiss me, but Patsy is staring at us, along with a few people on the sidewalk.

"See you then," I say. "Thank you for lunch."

"You're welcome. I'm really looking forward to tomorrow night."

"Me too." Beaming, I go into the office and tell Patsy every single detail.

PIERRE

It's the day of table reads—one of the most critical days of filmmaking, as it sets the tone for the entire production—and I am dragging.

After having lunch with Kendall yesterday, I couldn't think of anything else. I walked around the grocery store for an hour, debating what to cook for her before settling on gourmet pizza. Then I couldn't sleep. Then I almost forgot to eat breakfast.

I can honestly say I've never been this nervous about a date in my entire life.

Table reads are being held at the local library off Main Street. Though two stories, the library is relatively small. It's a brown brick building that looks at least a hundred years old. It even has the original windows with little blocks of yellow and pink stained glass around the edges. There is one librarian at the desk who looks completely starstruck when I walk in with a few other recognizable faces. A little sign indicates that table reads are upstairs, so that's where we all head.

The second floor of the building consists of three small conference rooms to the right of the stairs and a large auditorium with a stage to the left. I walk into the auditorium, where the edge of the stage is being used as a table to hold scripts. A circle of tables takes up most of the room. A few people greet me when I walk in, then I find my name card—right next to Marina's—and sit down. In front of me is a fresh script, two ink pens, and a bottle of water.

Marina isn't here yet. The last time we worked together, she was always late. I have no reason to think this shoot will be any different.

It's past time to get started and everyone gets settled in their chairs. The director, Belladonna, calls Marina and yells at her on speakerphone in front of the entire cast. Marina assures her she's almost here, and though I'm annoyed by her tardiness, I also dread her walking in the door.

We continue to wait, so I get up and stretch my legs. Out the window of antique rippled glass, I see a long black car pull up and Marina steps out, wearing a white tank top, beige pants, and enough jewelry to make the King of England jealous. I have to admit that she is attractive in that cookie-cutter Hollywood way. She has long, straight chestnut hair, wide brown eyes, fair skin, a sharp jaw, and she's almost as tall as I am. It's no surprise that all the major designers want to work with her. At the height of her modeling career, you couldn't open a magazine without seeing her in an ad.

I go back to my chair and take a sip of water. When Marina finally appears, she walks to her seat beside me without so much as apologizing or even acknowledging anyone else. Belladonna welcomes her in a tone dripping with sarcasm and we finally begin.

After introductions and the director's speech setting expectations, we settle into the rhythm of the dialogue. Marina is a great actress, which is reassuring. When we are delivering lines to each other I am careful to avoid her gaze —I'll save that for the camera—though she looks at me with an intensity that could burn a hole in the side of my face.

We break for lunch at noon and a caterer comes in with a spread of rosemary chicken, smothered pork chops, collard greens, squash casserole, mashed potatoes, and enough buttered rolls to feed the entire town.

I fix my plate and return to my seat, scrolling through the news on my phone, when Marina finally decides to speak to me.

"I've been telling myself you must've lost your phone, but clearly I was mistaken." Her voice sends chills down my spine.

I sigh. "Marina, I've been busy. I'm seeing someone, and I'm not interested in you."

She made a noise of disgust. "Don't flatter yourself. I was only calling because I was bored and wanted to go over lines."

"Well, that's why we're here today, so…"

She cuts me off. "Who is this girlfriend? She must not be anybody or I would've heard about it. You know the studio wants us to stage some pictures for them to leak to the media. They're not going to like you being seen out with some rando."

"She's not officially my girlfriend yet, and please don't call her a rando. Let's keep this project strictly business. I'm not interested in staging photos with you or pretending to be something I'm not, nor something we're not."

She sits back and crosses her arms, her leg shaking in frustration.

"Is she here?"

"Who?"

"Your non-girlfriend." She pouts like a child.

"None of your business."

"What's her name?"

"Marina—"

"Oh, she's Marina too?" she says sarcastically. "You have a thing for girls named after me? How sweet."

I finally stop talking to her and pretend she doesn't exist. We get through the rest of the day without any further snark, and when the table reads are done that afternoon, I slip away as fast as I can before she can say anything else or try to follow me home.

’ve been a nervous wreck all day.

Yesterday, Patsy and I went back to Cotton Blossoms before she picked up her boys from her mom's house so we could purchase yet another outfit for me to wear. Part of this feels a bit disingenuous, putting this much effort into my appearance when I don't even do that on a daily basis, but I still feel like I'm trying to make up for the fact that Pierre basically saw me after I'd rolled out of bed when we met. Maybe if I look extra put together from here on out, he'll forget what I look like before I've brushed my hair in the morning.

The dress we choose is red and white paisley. No shoes this time, since we'll be at my apartment. I do, however, get a manicure and pedicure so my nails are in good shape.

About an hour before Pierre is scheduled to arrive, I do my makeup and hair, then collapse on the couch and look around. I wish I'd put more effort into the decor of this place. I have a queen bed with a sage comforter and the chifforobe. On the opposite side is a small couch from IKEA and a TV. Apart from the long gray curtains over the nearly floor-length windows, there isn't anything on the walls and, aside from some photos with my parents and a few with Patsy and our friends Micah and Sistine on a side table, I've done basically nothing to make this place feel homey.

It's too late to worry about that now.

Finally, I hear the door buzzer. I check my face one last time in the bathroom mirror, then bounce downstairs to let Pierre in. He's wearing a dark green polo with only one button fastened and tan shorts. The color of his shirt makes his blue eyes look more emerald. I sigh. It should be a sin for any man to be this gorgeous.

After the usual hellos, I grab some of the grocery bags and show him upstairs.

"You weren't kidding about the tiny kitchen," he says, setting the food down on the stove.

I cringe. Now I'm regretting letting him come over.

"I—"

"Don't apologize."

I pause. He totally called me out on that. "I wasn't going to," I lie.

"Yes, you were." He smiles, showing off his dimples.

"Okay, you're right. I just don't have a great setup for cooking."

"It's fine. We'll make it work." He starts to unpack the bags—loads of vegetables, cheese, wine—and I suddenly realize I forgot to eat lunch. I am starving.

"What are we having?" I ask.

"I decided to keep it simple with pizza. I got store-bought dough since you said the kitchen was small."

"Good thinking."

He pulls out two bottles of wine from brown paper bags. "Red and white," he says. "I wasn't sure which you'd prefer."

"White," I say, taking the chilled bottle and putting it in the fridge to save for later.

He laughs. "You do have a knife and pizza pan, right?"

"Yes, but not much else." I get the pizza pan from the drawer under the stove and retrieve the knife from the one kitchen drawer I have. "What do you want me to do?" I ask.

"Talk to me."

I ask about his day and he tells me how the table reads went. Apparently, Marina was late, and there's pressure on him from the studio to pretend to date her for publicity. I feel a pang in my gut when he adds that last bit. I can't compete with someone like her.

His phone buzzes while he's cooking and I see her name flash on the screen before he silences and pockets it.

"What are you going to do about the studio wanting you to pretend to date?" I ask, watching him cut up mushrooms and peppers.

"Ignore them. There's not much they can do about it. Dating Marina is not in my contract. Besides, there's someone else I want to date, and any inch I budge on the whole Marina thing could jeopardize that."

"Oh!" I say, feigning ignorance. "Who's the lucky lady?"

He smirks and cuts his eyes to me. He's moved on to chopping onions and he's teary. Even my eyes are twinging a little and I'm not the one standing over them. He tries wiping his face with his tight shirt sleeve, but his cheeks are still wet. Without thinking, I reach up to wipe the tears from his skin. We're so close I can feel him breathing. I move my hand away slightly, then change my mind and return it to his face.

You can do this, I tell myself. *It's time to move on. This is a guy you like. Just go with it.*

We lock eyes and he turns his body towards me. Wrapping his hands around my waist, he bends down to kiss me. When our lips touch, I feel jolts of electricity run through my body and out the tips of my toes.

He pulls back and stands up straight, never taking his eyes off me.

"Was that okay?" he asks.

I nod, too stunned to say anything. My lips are still tingling and my skin is prickling with goosebumps. That was magical, like a bomb went off inside my body.

He leans for another kiss. This time I wrap my arms around him and pull him in, so close I have to remind myself to breathe. We're lost in the moment and the whole world falls away.

A loud rumble cuts the silence of the room—my stomach screaming for food. I can't believe I forgot to eat lunch.

Pierre pulls away and looks at me with a quizzical expression. "Are you okay?"

I blush. "I'm fine. I didn't eat lunch. I'm s—"

He raises his eyebrows like a parent about to scold a child.

"I'm so not going to apologize?"

He laughs. "Good. Now if you'd keep your hands off me, I could make this pizza and get you fed."

I know my face is bright red despite the makeup. "Fair enough."

I lean against the fridge and watch him finish chopping the veggies. Once he's done, he spreads the dough across the pan, swirls some jarred pizza sauce over it, and sprinkles on a generous layer of three different cheeses before topping it with veggies, fresh basil, seasonings, and ham.

"You'll have to come visit me in California," he says. "My house has a huge kitchen. I'll make you a meal that would make Gordon Ramsey jealous. When I do pizza, it's all from scratch. The dough, the sauce, basil from my garden, you name it."

I know he means well, but a sense of dread settles over me at the mention of California. For a moment, I had allowed myself to get lost in our little bubble, with him here in my apartment, in my hometown. As soon as he reminds me he doesn't belong here, that bubble bursts and I remember he's leaving soon.

"Don't say that," I say without thinking.

He's taken aback, jarred by the stern tone in my voice.

"Say what?"

I close my eyes and shake my head. "Don't talk about me going to California like we have some kind of future."

He nods but says nothing. Right on time, the oven signals it's preheated. He puts in the pizza and turns his attention back to me.

"I understand," he says. "I wasn't trying to imply

anything or get ahead of myself. I had this image of us in my kitchen, laughing, having a good time, and I wanted to share it with you."

I nod. "It's okay. I'm trying to be realistic and protect myself. I like you. I really do. But if I'm going to have you here and let you dip into my life, I have to see this as a temporary, fun, short-term thing. You don't live here. You occupy this entirely different world so foreign to me I can't possibly imagine myself in it. And that's okay. Let's enjoy each other now and not talk about the future. Once you leave, that's it."

"I understand," he says. We embrace again. "Why don't we open the wine?"

"That's a great idea," I say. "Glasses are above the stove."

He reaches up and pulls down the two wine glasses I have. One is hot pink and has "21" on it. The other is painted with my name and carnation pink polka dots.

"They were gifts from Patsy when I was in college," I say. "I can't bring myself to get rid of them, even if they are a little juvenile." Honestly, they have more personality than anything in my apartment.

"I love them," he says. "I want 21."

"It's all yours."

I retrieve the wine opener from a box under the sink and hand it to him. He grabs the white wine from the fridge and opens each bottle, pouring red for himself and white for me.

He holds up his glass to toast. "To us. To friendship. And to fitting in as many kisses as we can while I'm here."

I'm grinning ear to ear. "I like that." Our glasses clink and we each take a sip.

I settle on the couch while Pierre walks around my apartment, looking at the few photos I have on display. He stops at one of me in pigtails, wearing a lavender and white seersucker dress, standing in front of a giant rose bush.

"Oh, this is too cute," he says, picking it up.

"Yeah, that was in front of my parents' house one Easter before church."

"Do they still have that house?"

"No, they sold it when they retired to Florida. It broke my heart to say goodbye to that place. It was the perfect home to spend a childhood. My dad and grandpa planted the roses around the porch when I was a baby. A guy I went to high school with actually lives there now, and the roses are still there. I can't smell roses without thinking of playing in the yard as a little kid."

He smiles and puts the picture back. I turn on my Bluetooth speaker and Taylor Swift's "Wildest Dreams" is the first song to play.

"Taylor Swift, huh?"

"I love her."

"What's your favorite Taylor song?"

"Oh goodness. That's hard." I bite my bottom lip and glance up to the ceiling. "Probably the extended 'All Too Well.' Though this one is a bit apropos."

"That's a good one! I'm partial to 'Exile.'"

"I love that song! I didn't take you to be a Swiftie."

"I have this theory that everyone loves Taylor Swift,

even if it's in secret. She's a great songwriter. I met her once."

"No way!"

"Yeah, it was at a movie premiere. She'd done a song for the soundtrack and I had a film coming out with the same studio that year, so I had to make an appearance. She was sweet. We have some mutual friends. I've heard nothing but good things about her."

"Wow," I say, shaking my head. "Different worlds."

"Let's not talk about that anymore." He takes my wine glass from me, puts both mine and his on the coffee table, then leans in to kiss me.

Our lips are locked until the oven timer goes off.

I get up and grab plates while he takes out the pizza. It smells like Italian heaven and my stomach gives another roar, which makes Pierre laugh.

"Pizza cutter?" he asks, and I shake my head. He washes the knife from earlier and uses that to cut, then puts the slices on our plates. We each take one and head back to the couch.

The pizza is so good that I have a hard time being lady-like while I'm eating. Strings of cheese fall off the slice with every bite, and the basil fills my mouth with a fresh, savory flavor that makes my eyes roll back in my head.

"I could eat that whole pizza," I say.

"That whole pizza would not fit in your tiny little stomach."

"Wanna bet?"

I don't eat the whole pizza, but I do have two more slices. His phone buzzes twice while we eat, and each time he looks at it without responding. I don't bother to look to see who it is. I know it's Marina, and I can't help but feel a little smug. Perfect model-turned-actress Marina Breton is chasing a man who only wants me. It's as invigorating as it is bizarre.

For the rest of the evening we cuddle on the couch, listen to music, and talk about our favorite songs, movies, and books. Turns out, he's a total sap. Not only does he love Taylor Swift, but *Casablanca* and *The English Patient* are his top two movies and he's read *Don Quixote* so many times he can quote passages from memory. I feel a little uncultured when I tell him my favorite movies are *Easy A* and *Love Actually,* and the only time I read is when I occasionally download a romance novel on my phone.

I don't mention that my free time is pretty much spent streaming murder shows—that may scare him.

"Romance novels?" he says. "So, under all of that anxiety, you're really an optimist at heart."

"Maybe," I answer, cuddling closer. He's warm and, even though it's hot outside, I welcome the closeness. It's been a long time since I felt this comfortable with someone.

"You're not at all what I expected," I tell him.

"How so?" He cocks his head back and looks at me.

"I don't know," I say. "I thought you'd be shallow or narcissistic or something."

"Why is that?"

"Oh, come on. You know how you look. You're a movie star."

"I'm just a regular guy, Kendall." My stomach knots when he says my name.

"No," I say. "You're much more than that."

It's hard to leave Kendall after our dinner date. I stand at the bottom of her steps, kissing her for what feels like an hour. I could've stayed all night, but I know she isn't ready for that, and I do have pre-production stuff all day Sunday.

I call Harriett on the way home. It's late, but she is two hours behind me. I tell her all about my evening with Kendall.

"You're getting in way over your head. I've never heard you talk like this about a girl."

"I know! It's crazy. This definitely is not what I expected to find in Alabama."

"What happens after filming ends?"

"She wants to keep it light so we can part ways with fond memories, but I don't know. When I'm with her, I keep picturing her in my house in Bel Air. I want her on my arm at premieres. I want her in my trailer on movie sets. I just don't know how to make that work. I don't think that's what she wants."

"It sounds like she's not ready anyway."

"Yeah, you're probably right."

"Be careful."

"I'll be fine. I'm just enjoying it while it lasts."

We hang up as I pull into the driveway. Once I get inside, I strip down to my underwear, brush my teeth, and lay on the covers in the bed that once was Kendall's. It should still be Kendall's. This was her dream house and that asshole ruined it for her.

Hopefully, by the time I leave Magnolia Row, she'll be able to live here again, on her own, with happy memories instead of sadness. If nothing else comes from this relationship, I at least want to give her that.

Sunday is a blur of last-minute wardrobe fittings, meetings with the director about script changes after yesterday's table read, pre-production photography for PR photos, and a trial run of hair and make-up. I text Kendall several times throughout the day so she knows I'm thinking about her. She sends me a song on Spotify—"Daylight" by, of course, Taylor Swift.

I think of how awesome it would be to get tickets to her next tour and take Kendall, but I catch myself and try to focus on the fact that this is a short-term thing. Kendall does not want a commitment or long-term promises. She's made that very clear.

It's difficult not to think about the future with someone like her. She's not a short-term girl. She's a lifetime girl.

Marina, on the other hand, is a no-term girl. Throughout the day, she's driven me insane. First it was walking into my dressing room while I was changing during costume fittings, then she made a snarky comment about my phone working while I was texting Kendall. In our meeting with the director, she put her hand on my arm no fewer than twelve times, and during our still photos she squeezed me hard enough that I thought my ribs would break.

The highlight of my day is calling Kendall before I crash in the bed. She tells me she's thought of nothing but kissing me since I left her apartment. Since her office is closed for Memorial Day on the first day of shooting, I invite her to the set to watch filming. She declines, saying the town is already abuzz with rumors about us. Her parents even called her from Florida because they caught wind of our budding romance.

It seems small towns can be as bad as Hollywood when it comes to other people's business.

When I look at my schedule for the week, I don't know how I can fit in another date with Kendall. I'm going to have to wait until the weekend to see her again.

I tell myself the wait will make our next meeting that much sweeter, but I miss her so much I can hardly contain it.

Harriett was right. I am in over my head.

KENDALL

It's Memorial Day, which of course means everyone in town who is not working on the movie is on the river.

The weather is perfect. It's warm but not scorching, and it hasn't rained all week, so the humidity isn't too bad. Since Pierre is busy with his movie until Saturday, I accept an invitation from Patsy to hang out with her family on their pontoon boat. They live outside of town but offer to pick me up at Cattywampus since it's within walking distance of my apartment.

I put on my bathing suit, covering it with an Auburn t-shirt, cut-off shorts, and flip-flops and pack a bag complete with sunscreen, a pink ball cap, and a giant bottle of water. The walk to Cattywampus is short, and the easiest way down to the dock is from their back patio. As soon as I step in the door, everyone turns around to stare at me.

"Hey, Kendall!" calls Calista from behind the bar. "Where's your new man?" She winks at me and, though I know she means well, I want cover my face and hide. Instead, I try to laugh it off, wave at her as I go by, and trot as fast as I can down the steps outside to the dock.

When I get to the bottom, I stop in my tracks.

Patsy's boat is there, waiting for me as promised, but so is Tucker's. They're parked side by side and Garion and Tucker are on the dock talking. Patsy is on her boat, long tan legs crossed with a toddler in her lap and glaring at Tucker like she's plotting his untimely death. Her four oldest boys are running around, shooting water guns at each other and screaming, but she's completely tuned them out.

I take a deep breath and make my way to the dock. I brush past Garion and Tucker with my head held high, give them a polite "excuse me," then step onto the boat. I have to admit it was easier to face Tucker knowing he's aware of my new—albeit temporary—relationship.

Before Pierre, I would've cowered and called Patsy crying from the bar's bathroom. But now it feels different. Maybe I'm not the boring, unlovable little troll Tucker made me out to be.

Pierre f-ing Chatham likes me. A lot.

Looking at Tucker now, he seems a little ridiculous. His hair is too long in a midlife crisis sort of way, even though we're only thirty years old. I look to Whitney in the boat next to ours and I realize Pierre was right. She is a shell of a person.

At least she has built-in flotation devices on her chest in case of a boating accident.

I sit down beside Patsy at the bow of the boat.

"I told him not to talk to that f-er," Patsy says, her foot shaking in anger.

"It's fine. Besides, they've been friends since we were kids. I don't expect Gar to cut him off because of me."

"I do."

I chuckle. "That's between y'all."

One of Patsy's boys screams from the back of the boat.

"Archer, don't hit your brother with that gun! Guns are for shooting, not hitting."

I shake my head.

"Garion, we need to get back on the water before these kids kill each other."

Garion says goodbye to Tucker, gets back in the boat, and we pull off. As we're leaving the dock, I can't help but turn to look at Tucker and Whitney. Whitney has her back to me, but Tucker's eyes meet mine as he takes a swig of his beer. I turn back around, feeling smug.

Once we're in the middle of the lake, Garion puts an innertube in the water, helps his two oldest boys onto it, and we pull them around the river. Their lifejackets swallow their lanky bodies, and at times all we can see are the tops of their blond heads peeping out over the neon green nylon.

Patsy, recovered from her burst of anger at Tucker, turns her attention to a happier subject.

"So," she says, her excitement infectious, "tell me about Saturday night!"

"Saturday..." I say, tapping my lip with my finger. "I don't recall."

"Oh, whatever. Start from the beginning."

I go through every step of my night with Pierre—the pizza, the wine, the conversation, and most importantly, those kisses. His lips, his smell, his everything.

"Girl, you are in love with him."

"I've seen him three times. That's hardly enough time to fall in love with someone. Besides, he's leav—"

"He's leaving in a few weeks, blah blah blah. He's here now, and you are besotted."

I bite my bottom lip. "Okay," I admit. "Maybe a little."

Patsy squeals, garnering a look from her husband.

"I bet it feels good to see Tucker, knowing that Pierre f-ing Chatham is the last guy you kissed, not to mention the next guy you'll… you know."

"Patsy!"

"Whatever. You know it's going to happen. Admit it, though. It has to feel good."

I nod slowly. "Yeah," I say through clenched teeth. "Yeah, it does."

"I would say I told you so, but you already know I did."

"Yes, yes. You're always right."

She puts her arm around me and draws me close for a side hug. I put my temple to hers.

"Oh!" she says. "Guess what the second-best thing to happen with this movie coming to town is?"

"What's that?"

"They actually do need locals for extras! The newspaper posted it online. One day next week, they need kids for a scene at the baseball fields. I'm taking Gunner, Archer, and Buck. Then they're doing several days and nights downtown on Main Street and it says all ages, so I can bring all five boys. My mama and my gran are coming too. I'm so excited I could scream. You have to come."

"Nope. I'm good."

"What? You don't want to be in your boyfriend's movie?"

"He's not my boyfriend."

"He's basically your boyfriend."

"No, he's a guy I'm temporarily hanging out with who happens to be a good kisser."

She shakes her head. "Either way, I'm tickled that you're finally getting back to your old self again."

I grin. She's right.

"Me too," I say, gazing out at the bright sparkling water on the blue horizon. In the distance, a largemouth bass leaps from the water and lands with a soft splash.

PIERRE

This is the longest week of my life. All I want to do is get through this shoot so I can have Saturday afternoon off and see Kendall. At the same time, each day that passes is one day closer to me leaving Magnolia Row, possibly never seeing Kendall again.

I text Kendall throughout the day every day, then call her each night before bed. The days are exhausting. Belladonna is a great director, but she's meticulous and insists on shooting each scene in every way possible. I'm drained, especially with Marina right up under me at all times. She keeps trying to find excuses to be with me off camera, wanting to rehearse lines, block scenes, and presumably be seen together enough that we can spark those dating rumors the studio's publicist keeps insisting on.

The worst part about it is that, in the movie, my character is the one pining for hers and trying to win her back. This is the performance of my life.

At least the kid who plays my son is sweet. I try to spend my downtime between takes hanging out with him. Besides being good for our on-screen dynamic, it gets me away from Marina.

Finally, Friday night arrives. I walk out onto the back deck of the house. Bertha has figured out my schedule and is there waiting for me, so I retrieve a chicken from the fridge and hurl it into the yard. She slinks back into the muddy water as I take out my cell to call Kendall.

"Hello, beautiful," I say when she answers.

"Hey." I can hear the smile in her voice and it owns me.

"So, are we still on for tomorrow evening?" I ask.

"Sure. Where do you want to go? I'm afraid our options are limited unless we want to drive to Montgomery or Auburn."

"How about I meet you at your place, we have dinner at that steakhouse downtown, then maybe go to Catty-wampus afterwards to make your ex jealous."

She laughs. "Sounds like a plan."

"I'll text you when I'm done with the morning shoot. Should be shortly after lunch."

"Perfect."

The next day, I'm fidgety all during filming and constantly look at my watch. I send Kendall a few pictures from the set, which she responds to immediately. I love that she doesn't play games. I always know where I stand with her.

After work, I go back to the rental house, shower and wash off the makeup from shooting, then put on some clean clothes.

I drum my hand on the steering wheel of the SUV during the entire drive to Kendall's office/apartment. As I'm about to park, she texts that the door is unlocked.

I walk upstairs and she's standing at the landing, waiting for me. She looks stunning—hair curled, pink floral dress touching the floor, lip gloss perfectly matching her outfit. I grab her, lifting her and pulling her lips to mine. Time stops. Right now, it's just me and her.

When I finally put her down, she wipes lip gloss off my face.

"Hungry?" she asks.

"I was. Now I want to stay here."

She rolls her eyes with a smirk, grabs her bag, and we head downstairs into the hot June sun. Southern Star Steakhouse is at the end of Main Street. I put my hand on the small of Kendall's back and, for the first time, she doesn't tense or move away. There are a few people out and about, and though I feel eyes on us, I don't acknowledge them. Kendall notices, and I can tell she's uncomfortable as she tucks her hair behind her ears, clutches her purse, and never looks up from the sidewalk.

The restaurant is packed, half with locals and half with film crew. I say hi to a few people I recognize from the set, and even see my on-screen son with his real-life parents in a side booth. I introduce them to Kendall, who bends down to talk to my faux son about his Star Wars shirt. It's adorable to see them interacting and I can't help but imagine her with her own kid one day.

No, I need to stop. This is a short-term relationship. She's made that very clear. I do not need to think about her with kids or, worse, my kids.

Apparently, Kendall had called ahead and reserved a table in the back corner for us, perfect for privacy.

"I do their taxes," she says, scooting into the plush leather seat swallows her whole. "They don't normally take reservations, but for me they made an exception."

"Local VIP! And you think I'm the celebrity around here."

We waste no time looking over the menu and order wine—merlot for me and Riesling for her—and two filet mignons before I tell her about my day.

"Has Marina gotten any better?" she asks.

"Absolutely not."

"What's her deal, anyway? Can't she have any guy on the planet? She could be a model."

"She was, actually. Before acting."

"Of course she was." She rolls her eyes.

"To your point, I think that's the problem. She's not used to rejection. She can get almost any guy and usually does. Don't get me wrong—we have great chemistry on-screen, but off-screen I know her type. She's all about how the relationship would further her career, and I cannot stand that artificial b.s. I have no doubt she would tip off photographers and slip pictures to TMZ. Then, once the tabloid stories dry up, she'd drop me like a piece of garbage. So, yeah. Not only did I not pursue her but, when she pursued me, I turned her down. Now she sees me as a challenge. It's unbelievably frustrating."

She sits back, purses her brows, and shakes her head. "That's sad."

"For her, yes," I respond.

She goes quiet for a moment. "Pierre, can I ask you a question?" Her entire energy shifts and her serious tone gives me a mini surge of panic.

"Anything."

"Why do you like me?" she asks, shaking her head slightly.

"What are you talking about?"

"I get that you don't want Marina specifically, but you could have anyone else. Why me?"

"You're the opposite of everything Marina and those shallow Hollywood starlets are about. You're pretty in a way that's unaware and effortless. You're stable and grounded. You're independent. I can be myself with you without fearing that you have ulterior motives or will sell me out at the first chance. Don't get me wrong. Not everyone in Hollywood is awful, but everyone, no matter how good their heart is, is all about the industry. The industry is a machine. You're so… normal, and I mean that in the best way possible. I don't know anyone like you."

She gives me a melancholic look.

"Is something wrong?" I ask.

"No, not really."

"What is it? Your whole mood changed." I lean forward and reach across to hold her hand.

"It's just…I've never met anyone like you either. This whole week, I thought about you and how excited I was for tonight."

"That's a bad thing?"

"Well, yeah."

"I'm not following."

"It makes me dread you leaving. This whole thing is…" She pauses. "It's weird. I'm not sure how to define it. I thought I was above getting attached and worrying about definitions, but apparently, I'm not. Ugh. I'm so old-fashioned. I hate this."

My stomach drops. "What are you saying?"

"I don't know. I'm sorry I even brought it up."

"I'm trying to live by your rules here."

"I know," she said, squeezing my hand. "I appreciate it. You're the nicest guy I've ever met."

"Are you saying you want this to end?"

"I thought about it. At the same time, these past two weeks have been good for me. I guess I'm scared. Not just of getting hurt, but of not having anything to look forward to anymore. For years, I've been existing in a void with no horizon in the distance. You changed that in a startlingly short amount of time. I'm freaking out is all. It's a me problem."

I nod my head as she speaks and rub my thumb across her knuckles. She takes a deep, palpable breath.

"Can we talk about something else?" she asks, releasing my hand and pushing her hair back over her shoulders. "Tell me about your favorite places to travel."

I breathe a sigh of relief as the tension lifts. I'm glad she was honest with me, but I also don't really know where to go from here, so I go along with her change in subject. I tell her about hiking at Mt. Rainier in Washington state, flying over the Alaskan glaciers in a helicopter, taking my mom for a walk along the Champs-Elysées at night, and seeing the northern lights in Iceland.

She listens, enraptured, one elbow on the table and chin resting in her palm. As I'm talking, I catch myself almost saying things like "I'll have to take you there" or "I can't wait to show you this." I know she doesn't want to talk about the future, but all I want is to sweep her out of here and watch her face light up all over the world.

KENDALL

*D*inner is wonderful once I get my little meltdown out of my system. I honestly don't know why he's putting up with me. I'm all over the place.

We leave the steakhouse and decide to go to Cattywampus. I thought about going back to my apartment, but I know where that will lead and I don't know if I'm ready.

The walk to the brewery is heaven. The sun has gone down, the stars are out, and a warm June breeze is blowing over the river and into town.

Our table in the back corner is taken, as are all the rocking chairs on the porch. We settle at a high top in the middle of the huge room. I've never seen it this packed, especially with so many people I don't recognize.

"A lot of the crew is here," says Pierre after he orders our beers and meets me at the table. "Pussycat Blonde for you, Swamp Ass Stout for me."

"Thank you." I take a sip of my beer, wiping the foam

from my upper lip. "I figured they were mostly movie people," I say, looking around the room. "There are only a few faces I recognize." Of course, two of the faces I do know are Tucker and Whitney.

Pierre spots them at the same time. "Do they ever leave?"

I chuckle. "I guess not. Honestly, I never come here unless I'm dropping off some tax stuff for the owner."

"Oh well," he says. "Don't let them bother you. At least Marina isn't here."

"Yes, that would be..." I don't have words for how uncomfortable that would be, so I simply make a face. She's a model. Or was, anyway. I certainly am not. Never have been. Not even close.

For the next hour, we drink our beers, exchange stories from our childhood, and he tells me about his upcoming projects and all the new movies he wants to see, many starring his friends. He name-drops in such a casual way that I know he's not doing it to be self-important, which only reminds me of our drastically different realities. He goes to catered parties at Jennifer Aniston's house. The parties I'm used to involve a barn and a bonfire.

A few locals interrupt us while we talk to take selfies with Pierre, but for the most part everyone is polite and leaves him alone once they get their shot. He's gracious and polite with each person, making sure to ask their names and tell them how happy he is to meet them. It must get old, but he doesn't show it.

Then the inevitable happens.

Pierre is mid-sentence, telling me a story about doing his own stunt work in an action movie years ago, when all the color drains from his face. "Shit," he says. "One of the crew members must've texted her."

I know who he's talking about before I even turn around.

Marina Breton. Former Victoria's Secret angel. Cover of Vogue. Red carpet queen. Movie star. She may as well be seven feet tall. All legs in her beige miniskirt, flawless dark skin, hair flowing like she's fresh from a high-end salon, and teeth white enough to blind the sun.

Her face lights up when she sees Pierre. She waves like he was expecting her. He immediately tenses up and looks around, aware of the fact that her dominating presence has drawn more attention to our table. He clears his throat and rubs his hands nervously on his thighs.

"Pierre!" she says as she gets to our table. She says it like we were expecting her, then tries to hug him. He looks stunned, instead awkwardly patting her on the back.

"What are you doing here?" he asks.

"I heard everyone from set is hanging out tonight. Of course I had to be here." She scoots one of the barstools close to him and sits down at our table. She's closer to him than I am. He moves his chair towards me.

"I'm in the middle of a date here, Marina."

Not once does she look at me or acknowledge that I'm here. Even with him pointing out he is here with me, she pretends I don't exist.

"God, I can't wait to get back to California. The food here is awful. Not to mention the mosquitoes. I swear I'll be eaten alive by the time this shoot wraps. I'm surprised we don't all have malaria."

"Marina—" Pierre is agitated, but obviously trying not to make a scene.

"I think our reunion scene went well today," she says. "We have such good chemistry, don't we, babe?"

She puts her hand on his arm and rubs his skin with her fingertips. He pulls away, holding my hand under the table and squeezing.

"No, I don't think we do," he says.

She laughs, maniacally, in a way that's obviously fake.

"You're such a tease, Pierre. Always have been. That's what I love about you." With that, she put her arms around him and nuzzles his face with the tip of her nose.

I release Pierre's hand and scoot back. Everyone in the room is staring at us, a few with their phones out. This is bizarre to watch, but it's also downright humiliating to be a part of.

I take the last long sip of my beer, put my phone in my purse, and leave the table.

"Kendall!" Pierre calls as I walk away. He's right behind me, but I don't stop until I get to the door.

"I can't apologize enough," he says. "Let me close my tab and we'll get out of here."

I nod, then walk outside to wait. There's a group of guys I recognize from high school sitting by the front door. Of course, they're all chatting about Marina and how hot she is. They each talk themselves up, like they're going to go ask her out, but none of them even leave the table. I roll my eyes. So typical.

Finally, Pierre comes outside. He takes my hand, which I accept, and we walk back to my apartment in silence.

"I wanted tonight to end differently," he says, stopping at the door to my office. He faces me and puts his hands on my bare, crossed arms, rubbing them up and down.

I look down. "It's fine."

"No, it's not."

My gaze meets his. The streetlight behind me is reflected in his eyes, and he looks more handsome than ever. I wish I didn't like him this much. During the whole walk from Cattywampus, I try to convince myself he needs someone like Marina, that I should end it and move on with my boring little life while he lives his big, fabulous celebrity life.

I'm ready to say good night, but one intense look from him draws me back in and, before I know it, I invite him inside for a drink.

"I'd love that," he says, following me up the stairs.

I put my purse on an end table while he retrieves my wine glasses from above the stove. I only have one bottle, so I open it and pour us each a glass. We sit on the couch and I turn on the television, which is showing *Friends* reruns. I leave it there and sit back, leaning against Pierre. He puts his arm around me and I snuggle in closer, listening to his heartbeat.

After we finish our wine, he asks if I want him to go.

"No," I say. "But if you stay, we keep our clothes on. I'm not ready for all that yet."

Yet. The word slips past my lips before I realize the implication. If he catches it, he doesn't say anything.

Instead, he simply nods. After watching a few more *Friends* episodes, we make our way to the bed and I fall asleep in his arms. It's the first time I've shared a bed with someone since before I knew Tucker was cheating on me.

It's also the first time since then that I've slept through the night.

PIERRE

When I wake up, there's a wet spot on my shirt where Kendall drooled on me during the night. The morning light is streaming through the massive front windows overlooking Main Street, highlighting flecks of dust floating in the air like feathers.

I pull Kendall closer and kiss her forehead. I hope she's not embarrassed by the drool when she realizes it. Honestly, it's cute. I'm glad she's comfortable enough to sleep that hard with me sharing her bed, especially after how awkward last night became.

She moans a little and rubs her face, then sits up and looks at me with a sleepy expression. Her hair is completely swept over to one side of her head and last night's makeup has smudged into dark circles under her eyes.

She's never looked sexier.

"What time is it?" she asks, looking for her phone.

"Don't know," I say, kissing her forehead again. "Don't care."

"Don't you have work to do today?"

"Just a meeting with the director this afternoon to go over more script changes."

She gets up, last night's dress completely wrinkled from being slept in, and treads across the old wooden floor on tiny bare feet to the bathroom. Once she's done, I go in to do my business and search her cabinet for mouthwash. Waking up with her was too perfect to ruin my goodbye with stinky morning breath.

"It's almost lunchtime," she says when I come out. "I can't believe I slept that late."

"I haven't slept that well in years," I say. I put my arms around her, squeezing tight. She does the same.

"I haven't either," she says. "Thank you."

"For what?"

"I don't know. I just feel safe with you. It's nice."

"Yeah, it is."

"When is your meeting?"

"One o'clock. I should probably head back to the house and check my email. Belladonna loves sending me stuff in the middle of the night, then expects me to know what's going on as soon as I wake up the next day. The woman is a machine."

"Is that her real name?"

"Probably not. I think she wanted something that sounded scary."

She smiles and nuzzles into my shoulder. "When will I see you again?"

I sigh, closing my eyes and visualizing this week's filming schedule on my calendar. It's completely blocked off. I barely have time to sleep.

"Probably next weekend. I'm sorry."

"It's okay," she says.

"Next time, I promise no Marina."

"Yes, that would be great. You weren't joking when you told me she was crazy."

"She's the worst. I only hope the movie comes out okay."

"I'm sure it will."

I hug her tighter and she looks up at me. I lean down and kiss her long and slow, holding her face in my hands. When we finally take a breath, I close my eyes and touch my forehead to hers.

"I don't want to leave you."

"It's okay," she says. "You can't miss your meeting."

"You're right." I give her one last kiss, then leave her to drive back to the rental house.

When I get home, Bertha is waiting near the water. I get out of my car and run to the front door as quickly as possible, unlock it, and run inside before she can come around the house. When I walk to the back windows to look out, she's patiently waiting by the steps. Luckily, I still have a few chickens left.

Once I feed Bertha, I check my email. Six from

Belladonna since I left the set yesterday, and two from the studio's publicist reminding me that she needs pictures with Marina to leak to the press. I delete those last two without responding. I also have a how-are-you-and-what-is-going-on-with-Kendall email from Harriett. I respond to that one immediately, telling her about our dates and how much I like her, then go through my emails from Belladonna as quickly as possible before driving to her rental house to meet.

The meeting takes forever and it's dark by the time I get home. I don't even bother pulling up the computer. If Belladonna sent an email in the five minutes it took for me to drive home, it can wait until tomorrow.

I take a cool shower and lay on the bed in my underwear. I pick up the phone to call Kendall, but before I have a chance to dial, it's already ringing. Harriett's photo flashes across the screen, so I answer it.

"I thought I answered your email," I say as soon as I answer. We rarely begin with a customary greeting.

"Um, it's not about that." I can tell from her tone that she's about to tell me something I don't want to hear.

"What's going on?"

"Have you checked TMZ or your socials?"

"No, why?"

"You and Marina are all over it."

"What?" My heart sinks. This is the last thing I wanted. Not only will it encourage Marina, but it will hurt and confuse Kendall.

"Yeah, looks like you're at some kind of bar or something."

"I went to a brewery with Kendall."

"Yeah, she's in a few pictures with a sulky expression. It looks like you're just there with Marina."

"Oh my God." I sit up and run my hands through my hair. "Thank you for telling me."

"Are you okay?"

"I need to call Kendall."

As soon as I get off the phone, I dial Kendall's number. It rings and rings and rings. I leave a voicemail but don't mention the photos online. Hopefully she hasn't seen them. I send her a text telling her she can call if she's still up and, if not, I hope she has a good night. I lie back down. My mind races until about two in the morning, when I finally fall asleep.

Kendall never calls me back.

KENDALL

After Pierre leaves on Sunday morning, I lay back down in the bed. My sheets smell like his cologne and I simply cannot get enough of it.

I finally get up in the afternoon, go for a run around the historic district off Main Street, and come home to shower. I have nothing to eat, so I go to Piggly Wiggly to get groceries.

Standing in the produce aisle, picking out avocados, I see Mercuria Beaumont approach. I nod politely to acknowledge her without inviting conversation. We were friends in high school, and she still talks to Patsy on occasion, but she took a firm side with Whitney during the whole stealing-my-husband thing, so it's awkward. I'm pretty sure Patsy only keeps her around for gossip.

I look down and concentrate on picking out my salad ingredients, trying to ignore the fact that she's walking closer and closer.

"Hi, Kendall," she says.

"Mercuria. Hi." I try to act distracted by picking out vegetables, but she doesn't move.

"Too bad about Pierre, huh?"

"What do you mean?"

"I heard y'all were a thing."

"Um, okay."

She looks at me like I'm an idiot. "It's all over the internet that he and Marina Breton are a hot item now."

"He and Marina—" I pause, confused, my brain going in a million different directions. "Wait. What?"

She shrugs. "Google it."

With that, she walks off, leaving me standing alone and completely dumbfounded.

I shake my head, look at the grocery list in my hand, and concentrate on getting my things and going home.

Once I get my food upstairs, I leave the bags on the stove and sit on the couch. I pull out my iPad and open Instagram, then search for Pierre's name.

A lot of pictures come up. Mostly shots from red carpet events and stills from movies, but scattered amongst what I would expect to see are photos taken last night at Cattywampus.

Photos of Marina touching his arm. Photos of Marina sitting less than an inch from him, grinning like a crazy person. Photos of Marina with her arms around him.

I'm in a few of the shots. In some, you can see the back of my head. In others, I look sullen, staring down at my hands, my body language screaming that I did not want to be there.

The comments on the pictures are clear. Everyone thinks they're together. A few people had posted pictures of them from a movie they did together years ago and red carpet shots of him with his arm around her at the premiere. There are even a few shots of them talking on the set of the movie they're filming now. I recognize the buildings from downtown and the interior of one of the historic homes.

None of this is true. I believe in my heart that he's not lying when he says he's not interested in her. I was there that night at Cattywampus. The implication derived from those photos is complete fiction, probably fabricated and staged by Marina herself.

But I can't help feeling...gross, somehow. This is not my world, and the last thing I want is to be a footnote in some public farce.

My stomach sinks with a feeling of humiliation. I agreed to go out with Pierre to get back at Tucker – to rub it in his face that I could get someone better. And I did. The whole town was talking about it. I'd be lying if I said it didn't feel good. The problem is, I fell for it too. It started as a short-term thing, and now I'm in way over my head. To top it off, everyone in town now sees me as a pathetic wronged woman yet again.

I call Patsy, but she doesn't answer.

Instead of doing the healthy thing and walking away from the internet, I keep scrolling. Past the photos of Pierre and Marina are pictures of Pierre and every other beautiful woman in Hollywood. It seems to go on forever. They're all so tall, so perfect, so glamorous. I can't even pronounce the names of half of the designers they're wearing.

And here I am in cut-off jeans and a t-shirt.

I feel stupid. I know Pierre means well, but those pictures prove we're on separate planets.

This can't go on. I can't have any more pathetic pictures of myself end up on some tabloid site. I can't have any more awkward run-ins at the grocery store. I can't keep telling myself I'm okay with this being a temporary thing when I fall harder and harder each time I see Pierre. It's been good for me, I know. But I need to leave it at that.

This needs to stop before I get more hurt than I already will.

Patsy never calls me back, but I do hear from my mom. She's heard everything, of course, and wants to know what's going on. I want to confide in her, but since I know she'll just get worried and drive up here, I downplay the whole thing.

Pierre calls, but I ignore him. I don't know what to say, so I take the coward's way out and avoid talking to him.

I'm the absolute worst. He really does deserve better.

The next morning, I'm relieved Patsy is actually on time. She walks in, coffee in hand as usual, and rushes back to my office.

"I am sorry I didn't call you back last night. We were at the ER with Bow."

"Oh no! Is he okay?"

"Ugh. He and Buck climbed out of their bedroom window and onto the roof. They tried to sword fight with some sticks they found up there. Of course, he fell and slid right on down into the bushes. Thank God for the azaleas or he would've had worse than a broken arm."

"I'm glad he's okay."

She rolls her eyes. "Boys. It's always something. At least the pain meds calm him down. My mom is keeping him and Hunter this week while I take the other three to be extras in the movie."

"Oh. I almost forgot about that."

"It's still okay, right? You don't need me here Wednesday, Thursday, or Friday?"

"For work, no."

Her eyes narrow and she cocks her head to the side.

"What's wrong?"

I tell her about my weekend. The perfect dinner, my anxiety, drinks at Catty, Marina, seeing Mercuria at the Pig, the photos online, all of it. She sits while I talk, cross-legged and sipping her coffee.

"F that b. He doesn't even like her. He likes you."

"It's not about her. I want to go back to my boring little life. This is more excitement than I'd signed up for."

"No, you don't need to go back to your boring little life. Even if you give up on Pierre, which I don't think you should, you need to use this as a springboard to get out of your shell a little bit." She nearly spills her coffee while holding her arms up to feign a dive. "I've always known you can have any guy you want, and the fact that Pierre f-ing Chatham wants you proves my point. There's nothing wrong with being on your own if it makes you happy. Plenty of women live alone and are perfectly fulfilled. The thing is, it doesn't make you happy, Kendall."

I sigh and rub my face, then cross my arms and lean back in my chair. "I'm a mess."

"The first step to healing is admitting you have a problem. Good job."

"What do I do?"

"You know what I think, but you're a grown woman. I can't force you to keep seeing Pierre."

I nod. "Thank you for listening. I don't want to talk about this anymore."

"Anytime."

For the rest of the day, I try to concentrate on working and actually manage to get a few things done. Patsy sits at the front desk, gossiping on her cell for most of the day. A few times she speaks in a low voice and walks outside. I know that means she's receiving calls from people wanting updates on me and the movie star, which I have no doubt she diffuses as best she can. The whole town is talking and I just want to hide.

Throughout the day I get a few texts from Pierre, but I leave them unread. I can't answer when I don't know what to say, or even what I want. All I feel right now is confusion and guilt.

This is why I don't date. It only brings stress and disappointment.

Days go by. I text and call Kendall multiple times but get no response. At what point do I cross the line from pathetic to creepy and stalker-ish?

We were in a good place when I left her apartment Sunday morning, so I know this has to be about the photos, but she should realize it's all fake. She was there when the photos were taken. She knows the truth.

I can only guess that she doesn't like the attention, which I understand. She's not used to this. People post junk about me all the time. They always have. I know how to ignore it. She doesn't.

I just wish she'd talk to me.

The days are growing warmer in Alabama as we settle into June, and a summer storm pushes back filming sched-uled for the local baseball fields by one day. I spend that day catching up on email and talking to Harriett, who assures me that the end of this mini-romance is for the best and warns me not to let it distract me from the movie, but it's hard. I haven't liked a girl this much in...I don't even remember. Probably never.

The silence is maddening.

On Thursday, I show up to the make-up trailer stationed at the local baseball park as the sun is beginning to peep over the horizon. The sky has a glorious orange glow from yesterday's storm. Instead of being here, I wish I were enjoying the view from the back deck of Kendall's rental house, watching the sky change above the glittering river. I'm falling in love with this place. And with Kendall.

By the time I emerge from the trailer, the local extras have filled the parking lot and cars are lined up on the curb going all the way down the road. The air is hot and sticky from yesterday's rain, and I know I'm going to need multiple touch-ups from the makeup girl after I sweat everything off.

The extras are meeting with the assistant director near the central clubhouse. It's a mix of adults and a few kids, some dressed in baseball uniforms. Most people are still and paying attention, except for one little towheaded boy who is running around screaming profanities. I only have a second to wonder where his parents are before I see his mom run from the other side of the crowd to grab him.

I immediately recognize Patsy and my heart leaps. Maybe Kendall will be here too.

Who am I kidding? She won't even return my texts. She's not going to show up where she knows I'll not only be working, but working with Marina.

This is, however, a chance to talk to Patsy and find out what's going on. If anyone knows, it's her.

The AD breaks the meeting and everyone walks to their respective parts of the park. I start to follow Patsy, then feel a hand go down my back. I cringe, knowing what I'm going to see when I turn around.

Of course. It's Marina.

"Belladonna wants us over there," she says, pointing in the opposite direction.

"I'm aware of that, but—"

Then I hear Belladonna's voice booming from her megaphone. "Principals. Here. Now."

She's looking directly at me.

I sigh, look back to where Patsy has taken a seat on the bleachers near the edge of the park, and turn to walk away. Marina walks beside me, but as soon as I see my on-screen son I break from her and trot to say hi to him and his parents. He's dressed in a little baseball outfit with a glove that's larger than his head.

We go through scene blocking with Belladonna and shoot until lunch. Craft service hustles to get everyone fed and I stop to take a few photos with locals while we wait for food, my eyes constantly scanning the crowd for Patsy.

Finally, I see her. She has the foul-mouthed boy from earlier on her hip, though he's far too big to be carried. She seems to be taking it in stride, laughing and talking with some of the other moms.

I leave my place in line and walk to her. Her face lights up in recognition.

"Pierre! Hi!" She introduces me to her friends, and after I take photos with them, they leave me alone with Patsy, for which I'm grateful.

"Patsy, I hate to ask you this, but—"

"Kendall still isn't talking to you?"

I chuckle. Of course she knows. "No, she's not."

"Yeah, you've really thrown her for a loop."

"In a bad way?"

"Are you kidding me? You're the best thing to happen since her divorce. You're exactly what she needed. She's a little freaked out. That's all."

"What should I do? I really like her. I want to spend as much time as I can with her before I leave, but she keeps pushing me away. Do you think I should back off or keep trying?"

"She's not going to answer her phone." She puts her hands on her hips and bites her bottom lip while she thinks. "You need a sweet gesture. Do something to get her attention. Just not, you know, in public where she could end up on TMZ."

"Yeah, that was awful. I feel terrible."

"I doubt it was your fault."

"No. Quite the opposite." I pause, thinking. "Should I send her flowers? Diamonds? What do you think?"

"She's definitely not ready for diamonds, and they're really not her style anyway. Flowers are good. She'll like that."

"I'll do that. Thank you, Patsy."

"Anytime. And Pierre?"

"Yeah?"

"Be sweet to my girl. She deserves the best."

"I will. I promise."

She smiles, showing off the gap between her front teeth. "I gotta go wrangle these young'uns before they kick us out of the movie."

I laugh, then wave goodbye as she leaves. I check my phone. I have thirty minutes before filming picks back up. The line at craft services has shortened, so I grab a turkey sandwich, find a bench in the shade, and look up florists in Magnolia Row. There's only one. I call and tell them to send every rose they can find to Abbey Accounting as soon as possible, offering to pay if they need to buy some from a neighboring town. I have no idea how many I ordered, but it was stupid expensive.

She's worth every penny.

I'm in my office, working on payroll paperwork for one of my clients, when I hear the front door open. Since Patsy isn't here to manage the front desk, I get up and walk into the lobby.

At first, all I see is an arrangement of long-stem red roses so massive that it completely obscures the person carrying it.

"What in the world?"

A bright face with blonde hair and big brown puppy dog eyes pops out from around the flowers. It's Rileigh Briddell. I recognize her from dance lessons when we were little, though she's several years younger than me.

"Hi, Kendall!"

"Oh hey, Rileigh. What is this?"

"I'm working at Petal Place now. These," she says, carefully putting the flowers on Patsy's desk, "are from someone with very deep pockets."

"I can see that." She hands me a card, and I know it's

from Pierre without opening it. I stare at the roses. There must be three dozen in the massive white vase.

"Can you hold the door open while I get the rest?" Rileigh asks.

"The rest? There's more?"

She laughed. "Buckle up, buttercup. He bought out the store. If anyone in Magnolia Row wants roses for the next few weeks, they're s.o.l."

I hold the door, dumbfounded, as Rileigh walks back to the hot pink flower van. She gets another arrangement out and brings it in, then another, and another, and another until the van is finally empty. There are so many flowers that most of the arrangements end up on the floor. There's barely enough room to walk in here.

It's all I can do not to cry. He remembered the roses from the picture of me in front of my parents' house. The smell takes me back twenty years, like I told him it does every time.

Rileigh puts her hands on her hips, out of breath from hustling to get all the arrangements in.

"So, is it true?" she asks with a huge smile on her face. Her skin is so tan that it makes her teeth look bright white.

Immediately, I'm snapped back to the present. Here we go.

"Is what true?"

"Oh, please. Is it true about you and Pierre Chatham?"

"Um, I don't really know how to answer that."

"These are from him, huh?"

"I think so."

"Good for you, girl. Whitney's a real bitch. Nothing like

attention from a movie star to get Tucker crawling back to you."

"I don't want Tucker to crawl anywhere, especially not back to me."

She gives me a look that says *sure you don't.*

"Well," she says, "Enjoy these. They're beautiful."

"Yes, thank you," I say. She starts to leave. "Rileigh?"

She stops and turns back to me.

"Please don't tell anyone about this. I'm trying to keep this...this...whatever it is quiet."

She nods and walks out the door, leaving me alone with what feels like a thousand roses. At least it smells nice in here.

What am I supposed to do with these? I shake my head, overwhelmed, then can't help but laugh at the absurdity of someone sending me every flower in town.

Who does that?

Someone sweet. Someone who cares about me. Someone who is trying desperately to get my attention after I've been a complete flake and ignored him all week.

I reach for the card.

I hope you're having a wonderful week. I miss you and hope to see you again soon. -P

My walls come down again. I want to see him too. I can't fight it anymore.

I pull out my phone and take panoramic pictures of the lobby and my office, showing the garden of flowers, and send them to Patsy.

WTF. She responds. *I told him to send SOME flowers. Not ALL the flowers.*

You talked to him? I ask.

Yeah, I saw him at the movie set. You got that boy all kinds of wound up.

What did he say?

That he misses you and he wanted to know if I thought he should reach out again. I didn't think he'd be that dramatic.

He's an actor. That's his job.

Touché. Gotta get back to filming. We aren't supposed to have our phones out.

I "like" her last message and sit in her chair. What am I going to do with all these flowers?

I spend the next half hour hauling some of the bouquets up the stairs to my apartment. I thought if I spread them out it wouldn't look as overwhelming, but I was wrong. It's almost like they multiplied.

Five o'clock rolls around, so I shut down my computer, lock up the office, and go up to my room. I haven't texted Pierre yet, mostly because I don't know what to say. It was ugly of me to ignore him all week and I feel awful, but his stunt with the flowers worked. I want to see him.

I collapse on my bed and look at the pink and yellow roses on my nightstand. He really is the sweetest guy I've ever met. My dating and relationship experience is limited to one person, Tucker, who not once in ten years sent me flowers. The prom corsages his mother bought don't count.

I pull out my phone and text Pierre photos of the flowers.

Thank you. This is overwhelming.

He responds immediately.

You're welcome. I just wanted to let you know I can't stop thinking about you.

Do you want to come over tomorrow night?

Absolutely.

I clutch my phone to my chest and close my eyes. I can't believe this is my life.

Today's shoot is long and hot. It's outside at the ballpark again, so I have to go home and shower before seeing Kendall. I wave to Patsy on set, but don't have time to talk to her.

Marina, on the other hand, is relentless. She catches up to me as I'm walking to my car.

"I called you last night," she says, her hair bouncing behind her.

"Yeah, I finally blocked your number."

She shakes her head. "You're such a tease."

"I'm not teasing you, Marina. I don't like you."

She puts her hand on my arm. "We could be such a power couple. Like Jay-Z and Beyoncé. I don't understand your problem."

I push her away, hoping no one snapped another photo of us together. "That's it, Marina. You want the status. The headlines. The photo ops. You don't want me. You don't even know me."

"But I could."

"I'm sorry. I don't want to hurt your feelings, but this has to stop. Don't call me anymore. Save whatever feelings you have for the camera."

With that I leave, the heat of her glare burning a hole in my back.

I shower as soon as I get to the house. There are about thirty mosquito bites on my legs, so I decide to wear jeans to cover them.

I can't wait to see Kendall. It's been excruciating, not talking to her this week, which of course has only made me miss and want her more. I can't stay at her apartment too late. Since shooting this week got pushed back a day because of the rain, we have a full schedule on Main Street tomorrow.

As I'm leaving, an empty nail on the living room wall catches my eyes. It's about the size of a large photo, and I assume a wedding photo was there at some point. I look around. There are a lot of empty spaces here that once held memories.

Maybe if I could create new memories here, Kendall would come back. She said herself this is her dream house. She shouldn't let Tucker take that away from her.

I have an idea. Tonight, we'll make new memories.

"You weren't kidding about the flowers." I stand in the lobby of Kendall's office, the smell of roses completely overpowering as I look at the mounds of bright buds and dark green leaves covering every surface and half of the floorspace. I hug her and kiss her forehead.

"It's a little overwhelming, much like you," she says with a sly grin.

"You deserve every petal and more. I'm only glad I got your attention."

"I'm sorry to have you come over here again," she says. "I don't want any more attention, and there's nowhere to go without running into someone with a cell phone and a big mouth."

"Yeah. Even if we drive to Montgomery or Auburn, someone is bound to recognize me."

We walk upstairs, which is as covered in flowers as the office. I chuckle as she shakes her head. "I told you!" she says.

"I have an idea for these flowers."

"What's that?"

"Where's your camera?"

"At the bottom of the chifforobe. Why?"

"I want to take your picture. We can recreate your Easter picture by the rose bushes."

"I'm not putting my hair in pigtails." She crosses her arms over her body and covers her face, like she's embarrassed.

"You don't have to. I'd like to photograph you just as you are."

"But why?" She's suddenly awkward and putting her walls up. I can feel it.

"Because you're beautiful, and we have all of these flowers to use as a backdrop."

She flushes. "I— I'm not sure I'm comfortable with that."

"Why? You can keep your clothes on, I promise."

Her face turns bright red. "It's not that. It's… I'm not photogenic at all. You saw those pictures of me on TMZ."

I shake my head and walk up to her, holding her face in my hands. "Kendall," I say, "you're the most gorgeous person I know. Let me show you how you look through my eyes."

She sighs but doesn't say no.

"Besides," I say. "It's your camera. If you don't like them, you can delete them. No one else ever has to know."

"Fine," she says. She retrieves the camera and brings it to me.

"Do you know how to use it?"

I take a look. It's a top-of-line Canon with an L-series versatile lens. She certainly didn't skimp when picking her equipment. "Yes, this will be perfect. Turn on some music and I'll get us set up."

She turns on the Bluetooth speaker and plays a mix of Taylor Swift, Ed Sheeran, and Kelsea Ballerini. I move the couch against the wall and take some of the largest flower arrangements, setting them up in front of the coffee table, then put more flowers on the table itself. I take a pillow from the bed, put it in front of the flowers, then tell Kendall to sit on the pillow. The flowers behind her give the illusion of standing in front of a wall of roses. I take a pink one, break off the stem, and put it behind her ear, tucking her hair back. She sits still while I do this, her gaze never leaving my face.

"Don't move," I say.

I take one of the floor lamps from near the TV and reposition it in front of her, careful to position the shade in such a way that it casts a soft light on her face.

"Perfect."

I sit on the floor a few feet in front of her. When I pick the camera up and look through the viewfinder, she tilts her head down slightly, giving me a sweet, shy smile. I snap the shutter and she bites her bottom lip. I take another picture of her immediately before I lose that moment. She giggles.

"This is weird," she says, covering her face. "I'm sorry."

"Kendall, don't start with the apologies again."

"You're right, you're right." She takes a deep breath, pushes her hair back, and repositions the rose behind her ear.

I take at least a hundred more pictures. Halfway through, we each have a glass of wine, which loosens her up a bit. I get a few shots of her mid-belly laugh, which are my absolute favorites.

My phone keeps dinging with emails from Belladonna, so I put it on silent.

"Marina still?" Kendall asks.

"No, I finally blocked her number. This is the director. I'll check it when I get home."

She nods, then takes the camera from my hands and turns it on me. "I'm not used to photographing people," she says. "But it's only fair."

"I'm sure you'll do great. Besides, I have plenty of experience having my picture taken."

"Of course you do."

She snaps few dozen of me in front of the flowers, then I take the camera and we pose for a few dozen together. I even get some shots of her kissing me on the cheek and us kissing each other. They aren't centered as I would've liked when we look at them afterwards, but the imperfection somehow makes them more endearing.

After we get up from the floor we move to the windows. She pulls a curtain back and tells me to stand in front of the glass, then turns off all the lights so my face is lit only by the soft moonlight and streetlamps below. She takes a few pictures, which turn out moody and eerily sexy. I snap a few of her in the same spot, then she tells me she wants to shoot me again there, this time with my shirt off.

I raise my eyebrows.

"I said I wasn't taking off my clothes, but you said nothing about yours."

"Touché." I lift my shirt over my head and stand by the window again.

She takes about ten pictures, then lowers the camera and stares at me.

"What?" I ask.

"You're stunning," she says. "I still can't believe you're real."

"Come here," I say.

She puts the camera on a nearby table between two vases of roses and walks towards me. She looks elegant in the hazy light as I lean down to kiss her. She reaches behind me to close the curtain, then leads me to the bed. When her fingertips trail along my skin, my entire body reacts to her touch with a ravenous hunger that isn't fully satisfied until well after midnight.

KENDALL

When I wake up the next morning, bright sunlight is peeping around the edges of the windows overlooking Main Street. I pull the sheets up to cover myself and look at Pierre lying beside me, sleeping as sound as an angel.

He's perfect. Positively, insanely perfect. I cannot believe this is my life.

I look at my clock. It's nine in the morning, which is late for me. The music speaker died during the night and I can hear sounds from the street. There is a lot of chatter, vehicles going by, and a random, loud beeping noise, which is strange because none of the businesses on Main Street open this early on Saturday. I run to the bathroom to grab my robe, then tiptoe to peep out the window.

People are everywhere. It looks like half the town turned up for whatever is going on. I see cameras set up in the median, cars decorated for what looks like a parade, and in the middle of the road I see Belladonna. I recognize her from watching the Oscars with Patsy. She's waving her hands around, looking livid. Marina is close by, arms crossed and shaking one leg.

Apparently, they're shooting today. Only, there's someone missing.

That someone is snoring in my bed.

"Um, Pierre?"

He doesn't move. I sit beside him and gently shake his shoulder, then lean down and whisper his name in his ear. He rouses, then rolls over and grins at me.

"Pierre, are you supposed to work today?"

"We have a shoot tomorrow morning. Why?" He's so groggy he doesn't even realize it's daylight.

"It is tomorrow morning."

"What?" Now he's awake. His eyes fly open, wild, and he runs his hands through his hair.

"They're out there now."

He jumps out of the bed, not bothering to cover himself, then pulls the curtain back enough to see his director losing her mind.

"Shit. Shit. Shit."

I stand there, not sure what to do, as he pulls on his clothes in a hurry, shirt inside out, and checks his phone.

"Fifty missed calls. I forgot I'd put it on silent."

"I'm so—"

"Don't apologize. This is one hundred percent my fault." He sprints across the room and kisses me goodbye. "Last night was wonderful. I'll call you later."

I nod and he's gone before I have a chance to process what happened. I look back out the window and see him run out the front door, straight to Belladonna. Though I can't hear what she says, her expression is clear. She's pissed, drawing attention not only to herself but to the fact that he just emerged from the little accountant girl's office. Everyone within earshot turns to look at him, then up at me.

I throw the curtain closed and turn my back to the window, reality sinking in. By this afternoon, everyone in town will know that Pierre Chatham was late to set because he spent the night with me.

As expected, my phone is blowing up before I even eat lunch. First Patsy, who wanted all the details. I respond that I'll fill her in on Monday. My friends Micah and Sistine also text, and I simply tell them that I can't get into it.

Then, of course, my mother calls.

"Is it true that Pierre Chatham spent the night with you?" She sounds more excited than Patsy on her giddiest day.

"Mom, I don't want to talk about it."

"So it's true! You know, everyone in town saw him leaving your loft this morning."

"I know."

"I'm happy for you, sugar! Just one thing: he's not a scientologist, is he? Because you know how those California people— Wait. Hang on—"

I roll my eyes and hear my dad's muffled voice in the background.

"Sweetheart, your dad wants to make sure you're using protection."

"Goodbye, Mother."

"Kendall—"

I hang up. I cannot talk to them about my dating life, if dating is what this is. I have no idea what I'm doing. I had no intention of Pierre spending the night, but he was looking at me with such intensity when we were taking those pictures, and in the moonlight, he looked like a god. I got carried away.

Now I really don't know what this means to me or to him. I was apprehensive before, but now I'm a mess. I don't know what I want. Part of me is ready for this whole movie business to go away and for things to get back to normal, but that also means I'll never see him again, and the thought of it breaks my heart.

I'm in way too far over my head.

For the rest of the afternoon, I watch murder shows and eat junk food while trying to ignore the noise outside. Part of me wants to go downstairs and do some work, but I don't even want to be seen through the window on the short walk from the stairs to my back office.

What a nightmare.

Finally, that afternoon, after drinking the rest of the wine from last night, I take the camera off the table and pull out the memory card. I upload the photos onto my computer and go through them one by one.

They're perfect.

Even in my wedding photos with Tucker, I hated the way I looked. Here, I look radiant. No touch-ups, no filters. Just me. I never thought it was possible, but I do love seeing myself through his eyes. I'm so happy I let him take these pictures, and I'm grateful he let me turn the camera on him. He isn't a movie star in these photos; he's vulnerable and tender. He's the Pierre he only shows me.

Right on time, my phone dings with a text from Pierre. They're still outside shooting, but he wants me to know he's thinking about me.

I melt. I truly melt.

I dig a blank memory card out of my camera bag and duplicate all the photos onto it so Pierre can have his own copies. Once he's gone, I want him to remember me.

PIERRE

$\mathcal{M}$y stomach is in knots for hours after I leave Kendall's apartment.

Not once in my career have I been late for anything and, of course, today I am late in the most public and embarrassing way. Belladonna is mad, the entire town saw me come out of Kendall's door, and Marina has been on me like a hawk, wanting to know what's going on.

"What were you doing in the accounting office while we were supposed to be filming?"

"None of your business, Marina."

"Who were you with?"

"None of your business, Marina."

"Did you even spend the night at your place? I heard the studio rented some fancy house on the river for you."

"None of your business, Marina."

It's like this all day.

To top it off, I felt terrible for Kendall. The entire time I've known her, the last thing she's wanted is attention.

Now the whole town will be talking about me stumbling out of her place with my shirt on inside out. Last night was spectacular—she'd finally let her guard down in every way. I hope this morning doesn't set us back again.

I send her a text when I get a break between scenes. Luckily, she answers, which is reassuring after she ignored me most of last week.

Once I get back to the lake house, I take a much-needed shower after spending all day in the Alabama heat, then settle on the back deck to watch the sunset and enjoy a cold beer. Bertha is waiting, of course. I go back in, retrieve yet another rotisserie chicken, and chuck it towards the water, where I watch her disappear into the orange and blue reflection of the sky.

I crack open my beer, a Swamp Ass Stout from Cattywampus, of course, and call Kendall. I hold my breath until I hear her voice.

"Hi, Pierre," she says, sounding a little defeated.

"Kendall, I'm so sorry about how the morning ended."

She sighs. "It's okay. I should've thought about setting an alarm."

"No, it's entirely on me. I don't want it to put a damper on the night we had. Everything was magical until I overslept."

She's quiet for a moment and I find myself holding my breath again.

"It was," she finally says. "But we need to be more careful going forward. My phone has been blowing up all day."

"I agree. I'm just happy you're not mad at me."

"Of course not."

"Listen, I have tomorrow off. Do you want to do something?"

"Yes! I actually have a great idea for a date. No one will see us, I promise. Let me get everything set up and I'll text you the details. I also have a surprise for you."

"I can't wait."

After I hang up the phone, I take a long sip of my beer. I didn't realize how tense and worried I'd been all day.

I lean back and close my eyes, consumed with the memory of Kendall's skin on mine.

I wake up to a text from Kendall letting me know that Patsy and her husband will be at the house to drop off a boat around lunchtime.

My heart skips a beat. If this is her idea of a perfect date, we must be soulmates.

I pick out some light clothes to wear, then have a cup of coffee on the deck while I check my email. There are no fewer than five from Belladonna excoriating me from the day before. There is also a note from my agent about not getting a reputation for tardiness, and an email from Marina asking if she can see me today to go over some lines.

I delete them all.

At noon on the dot, a pontoon boat captained by a guy with a mass of curly dark hair pulls up to the dock. I walk down the steps, on the lookout for Bertha, and wave to him as he ties up the boat.

Patsy startles me when she comes around the corner of the house from the driveway, hair curled, wearing heels and a white dress covered in lemons. "Hi, Pierre!" she says. "We're just dropping the boat off!"

"Thank you! I'm looking forward to taking it out."

"Y'all have fun!"

I go back inside to wash my coffee cup when Kendall texts me to let me know she's outside. I notice she still doesn't want to come in.

The thick, humid air slaps me in the face as soon as I open the door to meet her. I pick her up and spin her around before kissing her. She looks amazing. She's wearing a white sheer cover-up over a pink bikini with flip-flops. Her hair is pulled back and she doesn't have a bit of makeup on her face. This is exactly how I like her—natural and effortless.

"I'm so happy to see you," I say.

"You just saw me yesterday."

"Yeah, but I was afraid the way I left and everyone seeing it would freak you out."

"It did, but I'm trying to get better at letting things go. Speaking of which," she says, digging through her purse. "This is for you." She hands me a tiny memory card in a plastic case. "They turned out really well."

"We took those for you."

"This is a copy. I want both of us to have them."

"Thank you, Kendall. This means a lot to me."

"Well, it'll have to wait," she says, "because I'm ready to

hit the water." She walks to the back of her SUV and pulls out a small cooler and a bag. "Ready?"

"Absolutely."

We walk down to the dock and get on the boat. Kendall drives since I don't have a boating license, and she looks like she's been doing this her entire life. Growing up here, she probably has. She's relaxed and in her element, smiling ear to ear as the wind whips her ponytail around like a propeller.

We pull into a creek and drop the anchor. It's narrow, but private and serene. There isn't another boat in sight, nor are there any buildings nearby. It's a thick forest of oak trees with masses of Spanish moss hanging from the branches. A few cranes dot the edge of the water, and nearby a family of turtles are sunbathing on a piece of driftwood.

As many movies as I've been in, I've never felt more like I'm in a fantasy world.

"I hope you're hungry," Kendall says as she digs into her bag and pulls out two sandwiches and some water. "I remembered your order from Bread Crumbs, so I got us some sandwiches."

We sit on the bench in the rear of the boat. Kendall takes out a water bottle and mists herself to stay cool.

"Do you ever swim in the river?" I ask, noting her bathing suit.

"You've seen Bertha. Would you get in this water?"

"Good point. Geez, I hope she isn't waiting for us when we get back. I didn't think about bringing something to feed her."

"Crap. I didn't think about it either. We'll hope for the best. Worst case scenario, we take the boat to Patsy's house and have her drive us home."

"Was Bertha there the entire time you lived in the house?"

"Yeah, pretty much. That whole area was wooded before they built the subdivision. She'd probably lived there for a while. Patsy's husband offered to shoot her for me, but I couldn't bear the thought of it. Besides, he'd just end up stuffing her and putting her in their living room. After a while, I got used to her."

"You know, you're right. I find myself assuming I'm going to need a chicken every time I walk outside like it's no big deal."

"Yep! She trains you to be her little human vending machine."

After we eat, we relax on the back of boat. We talk about everything from favorite movies to travel plans to embarrassing childhood memories to how many kids we want (we both said three). Before we raise the anchor, we even make time for some kisses… and more.

KENDALL

The sky begins to fade from bright blue to a kaleidoscope of pink, cerulean, and orange, so we head back to the house. I don't want this day to end. It was wonderful to be out with Pierre and show him my favorite spot on the river, have privacy, and let my guard down.

I like him, I really do. I decide to simply enjoy the next few weeks and not worry about him leaving, not worry about the entire town whispering about me, not worry about what I'm going to do in the aftermath of this whirlwind.

There are a lot of things I need to let go of, and my crippling fear of life is at the top of the list.

When we get home, Pierre helps me secure the boat to the dock and we start walking up the hill to the house. The grass is getting tall, and I make a mental note to have a landscaper come by.

I'm looking down, mindful of snakes, when Pierre

squeezes my hand so hard my fingers pop. "Shit," he says under his breath.

"What?" I look up and standing on the back porch—my back porch—is Marina. She's in a tight white tank top and tan shorts. From downhill, she looks ten feet tall. "Shit," I echo. There really isn't anything else to say.

"Marina, what in God's name—"

"You cannot keep ignoring me like this, Pierre. It's not fair to me." She opens the gate of the deck and trots down the stairs towards us. I don't know what to do, so I just stand there, clutching Pierre's hand and trying to block out visions of Glenn Close and pet bunnies.

Pierre closes his eyes and rubs his temple in exasperation. "Marina, you're insane. This has to stop. I don't owe you anything."

Marina approaches, standing two feet in front of me. I feel like a troll. She's like Medusa, all sharp edges and glowing brown eyes.

"You're really rejecting me for her?" She points at me, her finger close enough for me to bite, which I consider.

"I wouldn't go out with you regardless of whether or not I'd met someone here. Never at any time have I been interested—"

Then we hear a noise rustle through the underbrush at the edge of the property.

Bertha.

Of course.

All three of us see her at the same time, but only two of us keep our cool.

Marina screams like banshee, which only pauses Bertha for a second.

Pierre grabs Marina by the arms. "Shut up!" he says, but she doesn't listen. She's starting to hyperventilate between yells.

Still holding her with one hand, he reaches into his pocket, grabs his key, and hands it to me. I take it and sprint uphill to the house, only looking back when I unlock the back door. Bertha, knowing that I'll be returning with chicken, turns her attention away from Pierre and Marina, lumbering towards the deck. At this point, all I hear is Marina sobbing.

As soon as I'm in the house, I run to the fridge and grab a chicken, ripping the plastic off as I run back outside. Bertha is at the bottom of the stairs, waiting.

I hurl the chicken across the yard towards the tree line, away from Pierre and Marina. Not until Bertha slinks away does Pierre loosen his grip on Marina. She screams bloody murder in his face, then runs towards her car.

"You're all crazy! I can't wait to get out of this shithole town! You're going to hear from my lawyer, you little bitch!"

Pierre waves at her as she gets into her car and screeches away, then joins me on the back porch.

"Well," he says, "at least she's not going to show up here anymore."

We hear water slosh, look down to see Bertha easing into the water in the fading daylight, then burst out laughing.

"You'll want to wash your hands," Pierre said once our giggle fit is finished.

"No, I'm gonna go."

"Kendall, you're covered in meat grime. You need to wash your hands. Come on."

I turn and go back into the house. In the frenzy of grabbing the chicken, I didn't even look around or allow myself to think about where I was. I haven't been back here in years. Patsy always takes care of things for me when it comes to this property. My artsy photos are still on the walls, but she must've removed all the personal photos of Tucker and me. The house is cold without those human touches. I look at the couch and remember sitting there, crying for hours, after Tucker told me about Whitney and said he was leaving me. I remember vomiting in the kitchen sink from the visceral reaction of it all. I remember the feelings of humiliation and deep, profound betrayal.

All this must be written on my face because Pierre rubs my back, then kisses the top of my head.

"Come on," he says, leading me to the sink.

I snap out of my trip down memory lane and wash the chicken slime off my hands.

"Are you okay?" Pierre asks.

"Yeah," I lie. "It's weird. I haven't been here in a while. Everything is almost exactly the same."

"Kendall, this is your dream house," he says. "You told me as much. You should be living here, not in a studio apartment over your office. Don't let your ex-husband take this away from you. This house is amazing. I have half a mind to stay here myself."

"Don't say that," I say with a trembling voice. "I'm finally comfortable with things as they are. Just don't talk about the future like we have one. I can't handle that."

"Understood," he says. "But I have an idea. I want to do something for you before I leave."

"Okay," I say with uncertainty.

"Let's make this place your home again. All-new furniture, new bed, new everything. The only things that stay are these stunning photos you took."

I look at him, puzzled.

"It won't cost you a dime and you won't have to lift a finger," he says. "It's my gift to you."

"Okay," I say as he tucks me under his arm, squeezing me so tight I feel like nothing can ever hurt me again.

PIERRE

The next day we're filming downtown on Main Street again. I was planning to go into Kendall's office to talk to Patsy, but I see her outside with her sons at craft services, so I walk over to meet her.

"Hi, Pierre!" she says with a huge grin.

"Patsy, I have a massive favor to ask."

"Sure, what's up?"

"I want to redecorate Kendall's house. She gave me permission, but I don't have time with all the filming and everything."

"I think that's a great idea!"

"I need your help. Can you find a place where we can donate the old furniture, then I'll give you my credit card to go shopping for new…well…everything? You'll do a much better job than me anyway."

Her face lights up. "Absolutely! It'll be fun!"

I sigh in relief. "I can't thank you enough."

"Anything for Kendall. Thank you for taking care of my friend. You've been wonderful for her."

We hug, and she squeezes me so tight I don't think she'll ever let go.

"How was the boat ride?"

I sigh. "The best day I've ever had."

"I'm glad to hear it. We'll pick it up this afternoon once Garion gets off work."

"Watch out for the alligator."

"Oh, has Bertha been coming around a lot?"

I tell her the whole story from the day before, and she laughs loud enough that people around us stare, including Marina. I assume she knows we're talking about her.

"I said it once and I'll say it again: God bless Bertha!"

I laugh. "When did you say it before?"

"When y'all met. It was Bertha who brought you together, right?"

"You know, you're right." I nod my head, smiling. "God bless Bertha!"

That week, I talk to Kendall every day, and while we're filming downtown I take her lunch, which we share in her office. Everything with her feels comfortable and normal, like this is my regular routine.

Patsy arranged for a women's shelter in Montgomery to come pick up all the furniture. When I get home Friday, there is nothing in the house except the television on the floor and Kendall's pictures on the walls. In the kitchen, there's a brand-new air mattress boxed up on the counter with a note from Patsy.

Didn't want you to sleep on the floor. -P

Luckily, she left some blankets and pillows in one of the closets. I pull those down and set up in the living room in front of the TV. The new stuff is all being delivered next week, so I don't have long to wait.

Patsy enlists the help of her husband to do a lot of the heavy lifting, and texts me every day to tell me how much fun she's having redecorating the house. She's able to get everything locally, including some unique pieces from their friend Micah's antique shop. My bank calls no fewer than four times because of how much she's spending.

For the best part, I order prints of some of the pictures Kendall and I took at her apartment and the selfies we took on the boat. I pay for rush delivery, and when they come in, I give them to Patsy to have them framed. Hopefully that'll add a personal touch to make the place feel more like home.

I can't wait to see the finished product.

Saturday, I meet Kendall for lunch at Big Ol' Butts BBQ. My neck is sore from sleeping on the air mattress, but it'll be worth it to see Kendall's face when she returns to her refurbished house.

"Are you okay?" she asks after the thousandth time I roll and rub my neck.

"Yeah, I just slept on the air mattress last night. Patsy had the house emptied yesterday and I had nowhere else to sleep."

"Pierre! You should've told me. You could've stayed at my place."

"Are you sure? Don't get me wrong—I loved staying with you last time, but I didn't know how you'd feel about people seeing me leave the next morning."

"It's fine," she says. "I'm trying to do a better job of letting things go."

After lunch, I walk her back to her place, then head to the house to pack an overnight bag and grab my laptop. I go straight back to her apartment and don't leave until I have to report to set Monday morning.

KENDALL

Spending the weekend with Pierre is magical. I can't get over how natural it all feels, like we should be together forever. Sometimes I feel like I'm in a daydream and need to pinch myself. Other times, I want to slap myself for getting in this far over my head, knowing full well that his movie is wrapping soon and I'll go back to my quiet little life alone.

For the first time, I don't want that.

I wish he could stay, but I know he can't. Even if I ask him to, I'm afraid he'll say no. I need to do what I've said I would all along and accept that this is a short-term fling.

But, my God, it's been heaven.

Patsy continues to miss work since she's helping Pierre fix up the house. She assures me she'll be done by the weekend, which is good because I need her next week to help with end-of-quarter filings I have to work on for some of the local businesses.

I'm also a little anxious about the house. Our friend

Micah runs the local antique store and has apparently been helping her, which makes me giddy with anticipation because everything Micah touches turns to gold. I know it'll be exquisite, but I don't know if it'll make me want to stay there again, which is all Pierre wants. I hope I don't disappoint him or my friends.

In the meantime, he continues to stay at my apartment during the week. He's working on scenes being shot all through the night, so he's sleeping in my bed while I work during the day. Knowing he's a staircase away makes me feel warm and secure and gives me something to look forward to every day when I get off work. We always eat dinner together before he heads out, and each evening I'm left with a kiss on my forehead and the smell of his cologne in my sheets. Even when he's not here, it's paradise.

Friday afternoon, Patsy finally makes an appearance at the office. She's finished the house and is so excited she can barely contain herself.

"Let's go see it!" I say.

"Absolutely not. This was Pierre's idea. He should be the one to take you to see it."

"But you did all the work!"

"It wasn't work. It was fun!"

"We'll arrange a time for all of us to go together. How about that?"

When Pierre comes downstairs, Patsy shows him photos of everything on her phone, and a few times he looks like he's going to cry.

"I want to go now, but I'll be late to set if I do."

"Yeah, we don't want that again," I say.

We agree to meet at the house Saturday at noon. Patsy makes arrangements for her mom to watch her two youngest boys while Garion has the three oldest at the ballpark.

The next day, Pierre gets in at five in the morning and sleeps for five hours. I stay in bed with him and listen to him dream as I read a book on my iPad. It's been a while since I read a romance novel. I was too cynical to read after my divorce, but I'm finally in the mindset to allow myself to escape to a happy place.

We both shower after he gets up, grab lunch at Bread Crumbs, and go to the grocery store to get more rotisserie chickens in case Bertha shows back up.

"You haven't mentioned Marina this week," I say as we're driving through the canopy of oak trees in the historic district of Magnolia Row.

His face lights up. "Apart from being in scenes together, she hasn't talked to me."

"What? That's great!"

"Yeah, I guess after the Bertha incident, she thinks I'm nuts."

"Like Patsy says, God bless Bertha!"

"Amen to that."

Patsy is waiting for us outside when we get to the house. Micah is with her, looking gorgeous as always. She's about a foot taller than me, all curves, with bright orange hair that lights up her pink-pale complexion and green eyes. She always looks like a Botticelli angel.

Pierre introduces himself to Micah, grabs the bags from the grocery store out of his rental SUV, and we follow Patsy and Micah to the front door. It feels like we're the couple on a house-hunting show.

Patsy opens the door and I'm immediately hit with the smell of cinnamon apples. Patsy and Micah have spared no details, down to the air fresheners.

When I walk in, I'm swept away. It looks like an entirely different house.

There's an antique buffet table in the foyer with fresh pink roses and the plush leather furniture in the living room is covered in bright, happy accent pillows. Gone are the boring hanging blinds and in their place are blue and white watercolor paisley curtains. My photos are still on the wall, but the nails that once held wedding and vacation pictures with Tucker now display images of me and Pierre.

My mouth is on the floor. Pierre rubs my back and flashes that movie star smile as we continue to walk through the house.

The bedroom is charming beyond anything I'd imagined. Instead of the black Shaker-style bed and gray comforter Tucker had picked out when we moved in, there's a distressed cream four-poster bed with a sage floral blanket. The nightstands and dresser match, and there's a fluffy cream rug on the dark hardwood floors. It's delicate and feminine—the opposite of Tucker's style. This room, this house, is me. There are even pictures of me and Patsy on the dresser, and above the bed are the two moonlit photos of me and Pierre by the window in my apartment.

Even though he's leaving, he made sure he'll still have a presence in my bedroom. The thought makes me chuckle.

I grab all of them and we hug.

"Thank you. All three of you. I love it."

"Will you actually stay here now?" asks Pierre.

I nod.

Patsy claps and jumps up and down like a little kid. "You're moving back in?"

"Maybe. I'll commit to staying for a while and then decide. But the odds are good."

Patsy grabs me so tight I can't breathe. I pat her on the back, then struggle out of her arms.

"The extra bedrooms still have the cheap stuff you put in for renters," Micah says, "but we can redecorate those once you decide what to do with the space."

"I love y'all." I hug them again, then realize I basically told Pierre I love him in a roundabout way.

"Aw, sweetie, we love you too," says Patsy, but Pierre sighs.

It's probably for the best. "I love you" only complicates matters.

That night I stay in the house with Pierre. He cooks for me, properly this time since he has space to work. He makes manicotti with parmesan garlic bread and tiramisu for dessert. Afterwards, we drink a bottle of wine on the back deck, listening to the cacophony of whippoorwills, toads, and crickets in the distance.

At one point, I look over at Pierre, whose eyes are watery. He wipes them and I ask what's wrong.

"Nothing at all," he says. "I've just never felt this happy and at peace. I love it here. I love—"

He stops himself, and I don't ask him to continue. I know how he feels, and he knows how I feel. Saying the words will only make things harder.

I grab his hand and squeeze it. "Come on," I say. "Let's go to bed."

The next few weeks pass by in a blur. I spend as much time as possible with Pierre and sleep with him every night at the house. I even move my clothes there, repopulating the massive walk-in closet with the intention of staying even after he's gone.

Marina continues to leave Pierre alone, and though we see her out a few times, her venom is limited to dirty looks and snide comments to whoever she's with. Even the locals ignore us, as if running into a movie star at the local watering hole is a normal thing now.

Pierre and I do everything together, from grocery shopping to beers at Cattywampus to back porch sitting to watching murder shows on Netflix. Turns out he's a closet true crime junkie, too.

On July Fourth, the town has a big celebration in a park by the river. Food trucks come out, there's a live band, and fireworks are shot off from the bridge over the Florablanca River.

Pierre and I join Patsy and Garion on their pontoon boat with their kids to watch the fireworks from the water. Garion and Pierre get along well, and watching Pierre with the boys is so sweet it makes my ovaries explode. At this point, I think he would at least consider staying if I asked him to. He would walk away from his multi-million-dollar career and leave California to be with me if "will you stay" comes out of my mouth, but I can't say the words. I can't ask him to leave all of that behind. I tell myself that if he offers to stay, I'll say yes and that I want him to, but I won't go far enough to ask him.

He never offers.

PIERRE

Filming finally wraps on *Gossamer Road*. I have no idea if this movie is any good. I worry that the tension between Marina and me may have ruined our on-screen chemistry, but Belladonna seems happy with the result. Now I have to trust that the editing team will piece together something decent.

At least I don't have to see Marina until it's time to promote the film next year.

I push those worries to the back of my mind. Right now, I'm devastated to leave Magnolia Row. The thought of waking up in Bel Air without Kendall makes me sick to my stomach. I want to ask her if she would like me to stay, but I'm too afraid of the answer. Throughout our whole relationship, she's stressed that she only wants this to be short-term. She has been very clear on that point, and the last thing I want to do is put that kind of pressure on her and end on an awkward note.

In anticipation of leaving, I want to get her something to remember me by. She's not into fancy jewelry, but I did find a seller on Etsy to make a custom silver alligator necklace, which I plan to give her tonight on our last night together.

I call Harriett to make sure she remembers to pick me up from the airport tomorrow evening.

"Of course I remember," she says. "I booked the flight."

"Yeah, yeah. I just wanted to make sure."

"Are you okay?" she asks. "You sound down."

"It's my last night with Kendall."

"Oh boy. You'll be okay. Besides, she can always come see you in Cali."

"No, she's been very clear that tonight is it."

"Don't let her see you cry. I know how you get."

I nod as if she could see me. "I'll see you tomorrow, Harriett."

"Text me when you're taking off."

"I will."

I plan the final evening meticulously. Patsy takes Kendall to get her hair cut and nails done. While she's gone, I fill the house with candles and roses, though I did not buy every single flower in town this time. Her necklace is in a pink box with a white ribbon on the bedroom dresser. I even make a playlist of the Taylor Swift songs I know she loves.

I shower before Kendall gets home, and when she walks in, I'm waiting for her with a glass of Prosecco. I squeeze her tight and kiss her as deeply as I did on our first night together. When we unlock our lips, she's breathless and starry-eyed.

"I still have to remind myself this has all been real," she says.

"It's the most real thing I've ever experienced," I tell her.

She keeps me company in the kitchen as I cook filet mignon, baked asparagus, roasted potatoes, and garlic bread.

"Are you trying to put me in a food coma?" she asks.

"No, I'm just showing off," I tell her.

We're normally quite chatty, but this evening we're relatively quiet. She's radiant with her hair perfectly curled and the candlelight casting a soft glow on her face.

"This is the best steak I've ever had," she says after her first bite.

"Thank you," I say. "It's the butter."

That is the extent of our conversation at dinner. This is torture. I do not want to leave tomorrow.

After dinner, Kendall helps me clean the kitchen, then we go back to the bedroom. She sees the gift box on the dresser, but I tell her she has to wait until tomorrow to open it.

"Well, you'll have to wait for your present too, then."

"Kendall, you didn't have to get me anything."

"I wanted to. Besides, you shouldn't have gotten me anything else after the fortune you spent fixing up the house."

"That wasn't a big deal. I want you to be happy."

"It was a big deal to me."

"Understood." I embrace her and we kiss. She tastes like wine and strawberry lip gloss. My heart wrenches knowing this will be our last night together—possibly forever—but for now, I'm going to make the most of this night. Every inch of her body will get my full attention.

The morning I've been dreading for weeks finally arrives. Neither of us slept well, and I know the drive to Atlanta will feel like a whole day instead of three and half hours.

After we shower and get dressed, I give her the gift box. She opens it nervously, telling me she hopes I didn't spend too much.

"It's Bertha!" she exclaims as she opens it. "Oh, Pierre! It's perfect!" She's grinning from ear to ear and I hug her, pulling her close and kissing her forehead.

"Now it's time for yours." She goes to the nightstand, opens the bottom drawer, and pulls out a box wrapped in childish alligator wrapping paper.

"I'm sensing a theme," I say. She bites her bottom lip and watches me tear it open. When I see what's inside, I can't help but smile. It's a t-shirt from Cattywampus Brewing. "Kendall, thank you! I'm going to wear it all over LA."

"Good! I'm glad you like it. I thought it would be nice, since we had our first date there and all."

"Absolutely." I hug her again. "God, I—" I almost said

the three words I've been avoiding for weeks. I sigh. "I'm going to miss you," I say instead.

She pulls back and looks at me with watery eyes. "I know. Me too."

We don't speak as she helps me pack my bags. It doesn't take long since I had packed light. We load up the rental car and stand in the driveway for what feels like an eternity.

"I don't care if this movie turns out to be the most massive steaming pile of crap I've ever made. This was the best experience I've ever had. I don't regret a thing."

"Good. Me neither."

"I know you wanted things to end here, but please keep in touch."

"We'll see," she says, then bites her bottom lip. "I need to see how I feel once you're gone. You've changed everything for me, for the better. Before you came, I was a ghost."

"And now?"

"Now I want to reimagine my future. Set some goals. Evaluate my priorities. I need to decide what I want the rest of my life to look like."

I'm tempted to tell her to include me in that vision, but I stop short. She's made it clear she needs space, and I have to respect that.

"I wish you the best, Kendall. You deserve nothing but sunshine and rainbows from here on out."

"Thank you, Pierre. You too."

We hug one last time and I lean down to kiss her. I feel warm tears on my cheeks, which I'm not sure are mine or hers. She pulls away, face flushed and wet, and I realize they're hers. "Goodbye, Pierre."

I open my mouth to say goodbye as she turns away, but I choke on the words.

I simply get in my car, dreading the long drive to the Atlanta airport.

In the distance by the water, Bertha is sunbathing. Life will go on in Magnolia Row, as if I'd never been here at all.

KENDALL

$\mathcal{I}$ commit to staying in the house permanently and find a renter for the loft above my office to keep me from chickening out and abandoning the house again.

Patsy and Garion help me move the rest of my stuff, which I put in the spare bedrooms for the time being. I love that Pierre hung pictures of us together, but they make me so lonesome for him I can hardly stand it sometimes.

After he left, he let me know when he got to the airport and when he arrived home in LA. He even sent me a photo of his view of the mountains from his house in Bel Air. Every time I get a text from him, I "like" it to be polite, but don't comment. I also say nothing when he asks how I am, and I haven't returned his calls. I can't let this drag out. We both need to move on.

The town has gone back to normal now that the film crew has left. Movie chatter has dissipated, the streets are no longer closed, and it takes significantly less time to get a beer at Cattywampus, which I discover when I meet Patsy, Micah, and our friend Sistine out for drinks on a Saturday afternoon in early August. I haven't had very many proper girls' nights since my divorce, but the four of us hung out a lot when I was married and needed time away from Tucker.

It's a welcome return to normalcy. Patsy regals us with stories of the crazy things her boys have been doing, Micah gives us horror stories of her online dating experiences, and Sistine fills us in on all the local gossip she hears at the coffee shop she runs near my office. They casually ask about Pierre, but in a normal, friendly way instead of an oh-my-god-tell-us-about-the-movie-star way.

Of course, we see Tucker there. The weird thing is, Whitney isn't with him.

Patsy is the first to point it out, of course.

"He's alone," she says. We all turn around and look. He approaches the bar and orders a drink, but instead of getting a table, he sits on a barstool and makes conversation with Calista.

He looks around, sees the four of us, and waves. None of us wave back.

"That's weird," Sistine comments in her deep, no-nonsense voice.

"Maybe she's sick," says Micah.

"Yeah, with the clap," responds Patsy.

We all laugh, then go back to talking about our lives, but throughout the night I can't help but notice Tucker glaring at me unapologetically.

hen I get home, the house is eerily quiet. I put my purse on the kitchen counter and carry my phone to my bathroom to wash my face and brush my teeth. It dings as I spit my toothpaste into the sink.

I pick it up, look at it, and almost have a stroke when I see who it is.

Tucker.

Hey, just wanted to say how nice you looked tonight. I'd like to talk to you if you're free sometime soon.

I ignore it. I've gotten good at ignoring men lately.

He doesn't say anything else, and I go to bed. When I sleep, I dream of Pierre.

he following Monday I tell Patsy about the text when she gets to work.

"Mother f-er. What an a-hole," she says. "Of course, he wants you now that you've been with someone better."

"I don't know what's going on with him," I say. "It's weird."

"Do you think it has something to do with him being alone the other night?"

"Don't know, don't care."

"I bet he and Whitney broke up," says Patsy, pulling out

her phone. I know she's about to work her network of spies to find out what's going on.

"They're both horrible people, so it's entirely possible."

"I'll see what I can find out," she says, eyes glued to her screen and fingers moving so fast I don't know how she keeps up.

"Don't bother wasting your time," I say.

Sure enough, by the end of the week Patsy learned Tucker found texts on Whitney's phone from a guy she'd met at the gym. He hired a private investigator to follow her and, as it turns out, the gym guy isn't the only one she's been messing around with since they got married.

"Wow," I say when she tells me. "I guess people really do get what they deserve."

A week goes by and Tucker reaches out again, only this time he calls. I know it sounds pathetic, but I do feel sorry for him. I know what it's like to be cheated on, thanks to him. It completely robs you of your dignity and self-worth.

He leaves me a voicemail. "Hey, Kendall. I know you hate me, and that's fine. I'm not trying to get back with you or harass you. I'm going through some stuff and need someone to talk to. You're the best listener I know. Call me back if you can."

I wait a few days before deciding whether to respond. When I play the message for Patsy, she does not hold back.

"I know where we could hide his body," she says.

"Patsy, seriously."

"I am serious. In Cold Man's Creek, you can dump a body and the alligators would clean the bones before anyone would be any the wiser. That's why it's Cold Man's Creek."

"We're not killing Tucker."

"He's being selfish. You don't owe him anything. He's never brought anything but misery to anyone he's ever known. He's a scourge on the human race."

"That's a little dramatic."

"You're not thinking of seeing him, are you?"

"I don't know."

"Kendall! Do not fall back into this with him. If Pierre taught you nothing else, you should know that you can do better. More importantly, you *deserve* better."

I sigh and give her a hug. "I love you," I tell her. "You're crazy, but I love you."

After a few more days of thinking, I decide to see Tucker. Maybe I need closure, or maybe I'm curious to see how miserable he is now that Whitney's served him up a big dose of karma. Of course, I do not tell Patsy about my plans. I'll fill her in after the fact so she can't talk me out of it.

We meet at Cattywampus. When I arrive, he already has a table. It's early on a weekday before the after-work crowd arrives, and there's hardly anyone here besides Calista, who cuts her eyes at me like she can't believe I'm there with Tucker. He looks bloated, his hair longer than normal, and he has dark stubble on his face and neck.

He's already ordered a Pussy Cat Blonde for me, so I sit down. I keep my purse in my lap and cross my arms to make sure my body language is as uninviting as possible.

"You look amazing, Ken," he says.

"Don't call me that," I say. "Why did you want to meet?"

"She cheated on me." The lines on his face deepen and he looks at me with brown doe eyes.

"I know."

"Of course you do. The whole town knows. It's humiliating."

"Yeah, it is." My tone is sharp and accusatory.

He nods, then takes a long sip of his beer. "Now I know how you must've felt. I can't believe I did that to you. You didn't deserve it. You were nothing but sweet to me."

"Tucker, I really don't need your apology. I'm better off without you. It's for the best. Really."

"I guess it's easy to say that, now that you're with Pierre Chatham."

"Pierre is none of your business."

He nods. "You're right."

"Nothing in my life is any of your business," I continue, my voice calm but firm. "Not anymore."

"Look, I didn't come here for you to make me feel like crap. I just—" He leans back in his chair and runs his hands through his hair. "I miss you, Ken. I made a stupid mistake.

She wasn't worth losing you. Nothing could be worth losing you."

I stand up. "We're done here."

"Ken, think about it. You and me—"

He reaches out to grab my hand, but I pull it away. "No. You and I are over. Don't call me. Don't text me. If you see me out, turn around and leave."

"You think that movie star guy is going to stick around the way I will? He doesn't even live here. And he could have—"

"Me not wanting to be with you has nothing to do with him and everything to do with you. This was a mistake. I shouldn't have come here today. I hope you figure yourself out, Tucker, I really do, but you're going to have to do that without me."

With that, I walk to my car and drive home.

PIERRE

Time itself has changed since I got back to California.

My once-hectic, too-busy-to-think, onto-the-next-thing mentality has slowed to a halt. I still have a lot of obligations and things to do, but these are day fillers. I feel like I'm going through the motions and leading a completely empty, meaningless life. I miss Kendall so much it hurts. I miss Magnolia Row.

Hell, I even miss Bertha.

My schedule has been non-stop with promoting an action film I shot before *Gossamer Road*. It's coming out in October and the press tour is exhausting. I have upcoming appearances on every late-night show in LA and even have to fly to London to do Graham Norton's show when the film comes out. The publicist wanted me to do Saturday Night Live, but my agent was able to get me out of it. I'm too empty to be funny right now.

I wonder if Kendall is struggling like I am. I wonder if

she thinks of me as often as I think of her. I wonder if she's moving on with some local guy who won't leave her to go back to his career in another state after a few weeks.

I should've asked her to come to California with me. We should've talked about making this work, somehow. I have so many regrets, so many things I never said. I know I need to respect her privacy and her wishes to leave our relationship as it was, but it's excruciating.

My agent keeps sending me scripts for future projects since I don't have anything lined up after *Gossamer Road* is released next year, and there are some projects that sound interesting, but part of me wants to keep my life open, just in case.

In the meantime, I'm wearing my Cattywampus shirt every time I leave the house in the hopes Kendall will see a paparazzi photo of me in it and know how much it—and she—mean to me. It's my passive aggressive way of begging her to reach out.

KENDALL

onths go by, and I still feel the void left by Pierre as acutely as I did in the days after he left.

I still haven't talked to him. What's the point? It would keep these feelings lingering for even longer than they already are. He's probably moved on to another movie in another town with some beautiful starlet who will be comfortable going to parties with him at Jennifer Aniston's house.

I avoid social media completely on the off-chance a gossip site will post a photo of him. If I see him right now, my heart will break into a million pieces.

So, I focus on me. I read romance novels. I watch murder shows. I hang out with my girlfriends and go to Patsy's kids' soccer games. I even take a few trips to Florida to see my parents, which always turns into me dodging questions about Pierre.

The holidays approach and Patsy decorates the office

with a Christmas tree. I even put one up at my house, along with some porcelain snowmen and lights along the front porch rail.

The day before I'm set to leave for my parents' house to celebrate the holidays with them, Patsy comes into my office. She's wearing a Santa hat with a red and white striped dress and is holding her phone.

"I know we don't talk about Pierre," she says, "which is weird, but I thought this was sweet and wanted to make sure you see it."

"What?" I ask, and she hands me her phone. It's a celebrity gossip column site—all bright colors, sensational headlines, and the most unflattering photos of famous people they can find. It's trashy, several notches below TMZ. "What am I looking at?"

"You don't see the headline at the top?"

WTF IS A CATTYWAMPUS?!?!?!?

I burst out laughing and click on it. It's photo after photo of Pierre out and about wearing the Cattywampus t-shirt I gave him. There are shots of him grocery shopping, shots of him on Jimmy Kimmel's couch, shots of him in a director's chair with a movie poster behind him, all wearing that shirt.

The article is, of course, ridiculous. They're speculating on what it means and whether it's some kind of cry for help from the notoriously private Pierre Chatham. They wonder if it's a clothing line he's starting, or a liquor brand.

"Does he not own any other clothes?" the article asks.

"Perhaps he's so devastated after the leak of the sex tape of Marina Breton with a certain rapper-turned-music-mogul he can no longer muster the strength to change his clothes. Only he knows, and he's not talking."

I laugh hard enough that my eyes well up with tears. "I didn't know about Marina's sex tape," I say.

"Oh, honey. It's been all over the news."

"What news? Who cares about that?"

"By 'news,' I mean social media. Most people care more about that than they do the real news."

"Sad but true."

"Back to the point."

"Which is?"

"Pierre is wearing the shirt you gave him all over LA. He doesn't wear anything else. Have you talked to him?"

"No. His texts finally tapered off when I stopped responding."

"He's clearly thinking about you."

"Maybe his laundry lady or whatever servant he has is on vacation."

Patsy rolls her eyes. "You're impossible, Kendall Abbey."

She has a point. Maybe it is some sort of message. Pierre is thoughtful and intentional. He's not going to grab a shirt off the floor and go to an interview on television. Maybe he does miss me.

I sit back down at my desk and lay my head on the hard wooden surface. All at once, I'm flooded with a desire to reach out to him.

This is bad. So bad.

The holiday in Florida passes in a haze. Every moment I think of Pierre. I imagine him watching *Elf* in my parents' living room, talking to my dad outside at the grill, opening presents with us and taking selfies by the tree. I miss him. It's as simple as that.

I return to Magnolia Row a few days after Christmas. I dread New Year's Eve, but at least I'm not getting pressure from anyone to go to a party. Patsy is hosting a swarm of little boys for a massive kids' sleepover that night, and Micah and Sistine both want to stay in.

So, I stock my fridge with champagne and decide to spend the evening alone. Drunk.

I sip sip sip while flipping the channels back and forth between all the different New Year's specials on cable. Before I know it, I'm two bottles in and it's midnight.

I look at my phone. In the fog of too much bubbly, I pick it up, scroll until I find Pierre's name, and send a text.

It's midnight in Alabama. Wherever you are, I hope you're having a wonderful New Year's Eve.

As soon as I send it, I feel pathetic and want to crawl under the coffee table. I stand, stumble to my bedroom, and crash on top of my comforter, leaving my phone in the living room.

PIERRE

It's New Year's Eve and I'm at a party in Laurel Canyon. A ton of people from the industry are here, a mix of older artists who have been famous for longer than I've been alive, people my age who are here to network, and younger hangers-on who want to take pictures for their social media.

I know a lot of people in the room. I even consider some of them to be friends. I should be having fun, but I'm not feeling it. Not tonight.

I make my apologies to the host and leave early. It takes forever for the valet to get my car, but I finally leave and make my way through the dark, windy roads of the canyon towards home in Bel Air.

Then my phone dings. It's Kendall.

I'm so shocked and distracted I nearly run off the side of a cliff as I try to navigate a curve. I put my phone down. I can't look until I'm in a better spot.

Once I see a gas station, I pull over and pick up my

phone. It's a sweet thinking-of-you message, but it's like oxygen to a drowning man.

I stare at it hard for a solid minute, fighting back tears.

She finally reached out. This is all I've wanted for months and it finally happened.

I reply back.

I'm so happy to hear from you. It's a nice night but I'm missing you. How have you been?

Then I wait. And wait. And wait. I even go into the gas station and buy a bottle of water and some gum to kill time before I start driving again.

She doesn't respond. I finally give up and continue home. I walk in well before midnight, so I fix a drink and go to the back yard. My house is on the side of a mountain and has a panoramic view of the whole area. The stars are obscured by pollution, but the city lights on the horizon twinkle in the darkness.

I turn on the outdoor speakers, put on some Jim Croce, strip down to my underwear, and get into my hot tub with my drink and my phone. I look at the screen, willing Kendall to respond.

Finally, when my toes are pruned and it's after midnight, I turn off my music and head to bed. On my nightstand is a photo of us on Patsy's boat from the day we spent floating on the Florablanca River. It's the last thing I see before I fall asleep.

he next morning, Harriett comes over to drop off my groceries. I've just gotten up and I know I look like hell from a night of restless sleep.

"Jesus," Harriett says as soon as she sees me. "Party too hard last night?"

"No. I was actually home by eleven. I finally heard from Kendall."

"Not this again." She's heard me whine about Kendall so much over the past few months that I know I sound like a broken record. "What did she say?"

"That she hopes I have a good New Year's Eve."

"Drunk text?"

"Maybe? I responded asking her how she's doing, but she didn't say anything."

"She's playing games. You need to get over this girl."

"No, I don't think she is."

As if on cue, my phone rings and Kendall's face pops up. My heart skips a beat.

"Told you," I say to Harriett, who gives me a look as she unpacks my groceries.

I take the phone back to my room and answer. My palms are sweating and I nearly drop it.

"Hey, Pierre." She sounds like music, sending butterflies straight to my gut.

"Kendall, it's great to hear your voice."

"Yours too. I'm sorry I haven't talked to you in a long time. I've been sorting myself out."

"No, it's okay. I totally get it."

"I have missed you, though."

I exhale a deep breath. It's everything I've wanted to hear for months. "God, I miss you too."

"How have you been?"

"Good, I guess. I just finished all the promo stuff for that action movie I told you about. Pretty soon the same press tour will gear up for *Gossamer Road*. So, you know, work stuff."

"After that?"

"I haven't signed on for anything beyond that. I'm trying to figure things out myself."

"Well," she says, her tone lighter, "I guess you really liked that shirt I bought you."

I smile. "So you've been cyberstalking me?"

"No, Patsy has."

"Ah. Of course. How is Patsy?"

"She's good. Just chasing young'uns around as usual."

I chuckle, then we settle into an awkward silence.

"Listen, Kendall, I know we said we were going to leave things and let them end when I left town, but I miss you so much I can't stand it."

"I know. Me too."

"Can I see you again? I'll fly you out here, or I can go there while I have down time. Hell, we can both take off and go to Europe for a month if that's what you want. I don't care. I only want to be with you."

"Well, I can't go anywhere for the next few months. January kicks off tax season."

"Oh, yeah. Of course."

"But you're welcome to keep me company here. I'll be working late most nights until the end of April. It'll be super boring for you, but you're more than welcome to stay as long as you want and distract me when I'm ready to pull my hair out."

"I'd love that," I say. "I'll be your housewife and have dinner ready for you each night."

"That sounds amazing," she says. "I've always wanted a housewife."

"How soon can I come?"

"As soon as you like."

We end the call, and though I want to tell her I love her, I decide to wait and do it in person. I go to the kitchen, where Harriett has finished unpacking my groceries.

"You might as well repack all the food and take it home with you," I say.

"What? Why?"

"I need you to book me a flight to Atlanta asap. And drive me to the airport."

She raises her eyebrows. "Okay."

KENDALL

*P*ierre texts and says he'll arrive tonight after midnight. I put on my best lingerie, a matching black silk robe, and light candles in every room. The house is quiet as I look out the front window and wait.

Finally, I see headlights.

I watch as Pierre pulls into the driveway, parks outside the garage, and comes straight to the front door without so much as getting his bags. I open it before he has a chance to knock.

When I see him, he takes my breath away. I let out a sigh, not of relief but of gratitude. I'm grateful for him, for my life, for how overwhelmingly lucky I am that this amazing human flew all the way across the country to be with me.

He grabs me around the waist and lifts me as he walks in. I wrap my arms around him and we kiss until we both need to come up for air.

"I can't tell you how happy I am to be here," he says,

setting me down. He looks at me with such intensity that I feel like I could catch fire.

"I've been lonely without you," I say.

He looks at me and shakes his head slightly. "I love you, Kendall. I don't ever want to be without you again. I don't know what it'll look like, but I know in my soul we're meant to be together. I'll do anything to make this work."

I bite my bottom lip. "That's what I want too."

He looks like a weight has been lifted from his shoulders.

"Thank you. I love you." We kiss again.

"I love you, too."

"Come on," I say. "You must be tired. Let's go to bed."

"I'm on California time," he says. "I'm not tired at all. But we're definitely going to bed."

I hold his hand and we walk to the bedroom. As I close the curtains to the window overlooking the Florablanca River, I see Bertha sleeping on the dock and smile.

AUTHOR'S NOTE

This is a work of fiction. In no way do I recommend controlling your alligator problem with rotisserie chickens in real life. Please call a professional who knows what they're doing.

And don't sue me.

ACKNOWLEDGMENTS

Most writers will tell you this is the hardest part of writing the book, and it's true. It should be easy to sit down and come up with a list of people who helped you along the way, but the fact of the matter is that there are hundreds of people who deserve both direct and indirect credit for raising a book baby. Like with real children, it takes a village. Since the acknowledgments shouldn't be longer than the actual novel, this list will be woefully incomplete.

First I'd like to thank my friends who not only encouraged me from the beginning but also took the time to read my manuscript when it was in a very rough phase and offered constructive feedback: Lauren Lamey, Wendy Wason, and Kista Hamilton. I also would not have had the courage or know-how to even begin this journey without the support and inspiration from my fellow writer friends LaKisha Cargill, Jaye Robin Brown, Lisa Maxwell, and Ellis James. I am further indebted to Lexi Ryan for essentially giving me a step-by-step blueprint on how to approach this from a business perspective. Community is key, and joining my local RWA chapter, Southern Magic, has been an invaluable experience, so I'd like to thank all the ladies of that group as well.

This book would not be what it is without the hard

work of my editor, Karie Crawford. I've been told that good editors are hard to find, but I got extremely lucky when I found Karie. She spent weeks helping me get my manuscript polished and provided the feedback I needed to make me more confident in this story and get it ready for publication. Karie, I can't thank you enough.

My "co-writer" and four-legged baby love, Piper (aka Chicken, aka Stinky Butt, aka Old Lady), deserves thanks for always being a welcome distraction, keeping me grounded, and giving me the stink eye when I deserve it.

Last but most importantly, I'd like to thank my husband and best friend, Will. I can say in full confidence that this book never would have happened without you. I love you to the moon and back.

ABOUT THE AUTHOR

Anna May grew up in rural Alabama and studied English at Auburn University. She lives in Birmingham with her husband and a grumpy Yorkie. Wildest Dreams is her first book.

Be sure to visit annamaybooks.com and sign up for the Anna May newsletter to get more information about books, merchandise, and all things Magnolia Row!

instagram.com/annamaybooks